MURDER WITHOUT MOULES
by E. Arpajon

Copyright © 2022 E. Arpajon
Typeset by Michael Daye

ISBN: 978-1-329-05118-8

£1·50

For, in order of appearance, Kim, Orhan, Michael, Ellen, Carla and Ruby

Chapter One

Callery woke up and felt hungry. Then he felt happy (first things first). Today was the start of six days off. Off the tedium of case meetings, off stupid paperwork, off boring colleagues, off stupid bloody crimes and criminals – so depressing and so, so predictable. Today he was going to France for as many fantastic meals as he could fit in. Which would be a lot. As soon as he arrived he planned to take trains to Rouen, to Paris, to Versailles and make the most of his gastronomic trip. He probably wouldn't get further than Calais though; there were enough places to eat in Calais.

The B&B he was in was okay, clean and quiet and a short cab ride from the port. Fish and chips the evening before had been all right, although a bit on the small side – Dover's idea of extra-large wasn't Callery's.

He stretched and his feet clattered on the floor. Callery was still six foot four, still weighed eight and a half stone and still had the appetite of a teenage mammoth. Make that two mammoths. He wasn't still thirty-five though; thirty-eight now, edging towards forty. He ought to be obsessed with promotion, but all he was obsessed with at that precise moment was the idea of consuming as many oysters as possible in only a few hours' time. He pushed his body to the end of the bed and joined his feet on the floor.

After the Habbabenleigh case he'd asked for a transfer to the coast, somewhere near to France. Callery had a fancy to move to France permanently, some day. Well he'd got a transfer, eventually; to Dover. As near to Calais as you could get but a bit in the sticks town-wise.

Dover was small and provincial, with a similar level of drug crime to many other seaside places in Britain; an ill-fitting mixture of nice old houses and neglected ones converted into grotty flats. Dover was rundown, but so was Callery. He was determined to have a proper break and rent something decent when he got back from his holiday and started work. The B&B was fine for now.

****

Jeanne Torbet settled into the back of the car and smiled. The driver got into the front and started off. He was wearing a cap, good. A little old-fashioned, but Jeanne liked the old-fashioned things, the classic things. This drive for instance – she could easily have taken the train, but that would have been ordinary, what common people did. Jeanne did not consider herself ordinary. It was a pity that she was going to have to board a ferry to cross to France instead of a private plane to Le Touquet, but she hadn't managed to incorporate that little detail into her plan. C'est ça, no matter. She would be in the First Class lounge and another chauffeur-driven car would be waiting to collect her at Calais. A short while after that she would be checking into her hotel and her new life would begin. Jeanne smiled even more.

****

Seagulls whirled, screaming into the wind. The weather was fine, clean white clouds bustling across the blue sky above the port of Dover. One ferry was coming in and another was waiting to leave. Cars were being loaded, foot passengers were queueing. On the boat the crew was hard at work, either on the vessel itself or stocking up for the enjoyable crossing everybody was waiting to have.

Steve Sprauncey dragged two cases of wine along the passageway from the storeroom and behind the bar. The clinking stopped and Sprauncey groaned. His back was playing up again, sod it. He reckoned that there girl could deal with the bottles while he sorted out the till – standing work, that was, not bending. Plus he could get a good eyeful of her bum as she was doing it. Nice bum, she had. Tits a bit on the insufficient side, but pert. Steve liked pert. And here she was now –

'What you grinning at?' The girl shot him a filthy look. Steve stopped leering and tried to look stern. He was supposed to be the boss round here.

'I'll grin if I like, Ms Misery. Unload these 'ere lagers and make sure we're all stocked up for the next trip.' Nice bum maybe, but she was too chippy by half. Steve decided to go and see Becky once the till was straight. Becky ran the perfume and cosmetic shop and was always all right for a good feel up in the small cupboard that was her stockroom. It smelled nice in there, too.

'An' give over staring at my bum!'

'Oh stop moanin' Lauren, I'm not lookin' at your bloody arse. And mind you don't break any of them bottles neither; breakages is wastages, remember.'

Lauren groaned to herself. She hated Steve Sprauncey, hated his ignorance and his stupid Kentish accent, his lasciviousness and the way he obviously thought that every female who laid eyes on him thought he was sex personified. He made her feel sick, him and his stupid phrases about work. Any minute now he'd come out with another one: Get A Move On, Time Is My Money.

'Come on, get a move on – time is my money – ain't *that* the truth!' Steve cackled, bashed the drawer of the till closed and pressed past her with a sneaky push of his crotch against her backside. What a dirty, revolting, thieving bastard he was. Lauren jerked out of the way and threw Steve another look of utter hate. She'd shop him one day, she really would. But not until she'd stolen enough herself.

****

It would be stupid to spoil lunch so Callery had a small breakfast, just the five sausages and four fried eggs, no beans. Then he paid his bill and went to the ferry. Plenty of time. One ship was steadily easing out; the one he was going to travel on was waiting to swallow its load of people and their cars. Callery was just starting to get hungry when boarding started. Foot passengers swarmed onto the ferry, most with rucksacks or shopping trolleys – empty, ready to be crammed with Brie and Burgundy. Callery carried nothing except an excitedly empty stomach. He was going to find a decent little brasserie – the classic kind, gingham tablecloths and a zinc bar – and have a good, solid five-course meal. Hors d'oeuvres, moules, a huge steak and frites, cheese and then tarte au pomme. And a big carafe of the maison rouge.

****

Anishka Perry stared out of her office window across the driveway to the main road through Stuttenden. Nearly every car that passed was big, new and expensive; Stuttenden didn't do cheap or secondhand. It was a very wealthy village because of the school; the school was extremely successful and profitable because of the village. A lovely, mutually rewarding partnership – and Anishka Perry was the Head. How very, very nice.

She turned from the window and looked at some papers on her desk; accounts. A general summary of what the estimated profits would be for the last term, before school had broken up for the summer. They were lovely figures, full, pleasing ones that would mean a very, very nice increase in her salary. Anishka Perry thanked god for her brilliant accountant and his team and almost passed out with ecstasy. She was devoted to Stutters – the charming nickname used by pupils, staff and inhabitants of the village alike – and blessed the day four years ago that she'd been appointed Head. It was an easy school to run – there were enough ludicrously rich parents who'd pay almost anything to have their unacademic offspring bask in the success of the naturally clever ones. It was enough for them to be able to boast that Bella or Harley was at Stutters and that this year's exam results had included twenty Grade 9 GCSEs – Bella or Harley didn't actually have to be the pupils who'd achieved them.

****

Jeanne's car reached the port and the driver allowed her to make a graceful exit, carried her luggage to the foot passengers' pre-boarding lounge and tipped his hat in a respectful goodbye. She smiled faintly at him. He walked away; if she'd been a bloke he'd have been saying *what a wanker* to himself.

Jeanne tapped an elegantly-shod foot to show her impatience and rejected the thought of sitting down. She tried to ignore the other people waiting; she shouldn't be amongst these appallingly lower-class types. It was the worst part of her journey and almost fractured the beautiful life she'd constructed. They were fat, many of them, especially the women – except for one ridiculously tall, thin male who stood on his own in a corner, staring blankly ahead of him. Oh when were they going to be able to board this wretched ship, when could she nestle herself in somewhere called the Club Lounge – presumably the closest thing to First Class she could hope for – somewhere these chattering, snickering cretins would be forbidden to enter? And then, suddenly, boarding began.

****

Lauren had been to the bigger storeroom for the bar and restaurant, two decks below. Lugging three boxes of beer up the stairs had made her even angrier; Steve had told her not to waste time with the trolley and the lift, just nip down and get them. Nip yourself, thought Lauren, right in your fat arse. She passed bloody passengers on her way back, who'd surged up from the car deck; the usual noisy families, a group of lorry drivers, a not so usual incredibly tall and skinny bloke who looked as though he hadn't eaten for weeks. She reached the bar, groaning at the weight of the boxes and dropped them on the floor under the bar.

'Mind what you're doin', girl!' said Sprauncey. 'Them bottles better not 'ave broke!' Lauren glared. She was *definitely* going to shop him. And then people started appearing.

''Ere they come, the 'ordes – look sharp, Lauren.' Steve Sprauncey put on his professional grin as the first passengers filtered into the lounge, laid claim to seats with their bags and jackets and started coming to the bar to order. He'd just got back himself after a right good session with Becky in her stock cupboard – quick of course, but still very worthwhile – and now felt that he could give his best to this crowd, however demanding. He was good at his job, he had the speed, the deftness and the patter. Oh yes.

'Lauren!'

'What?'

'Are you all set? An' don't bellow what at me like that, you're my assistant remember – you assist *me*, not the other bloody way round. An' put a smile on yer – oh, good *mornin'* madam, welcome aboard an' what can I get you?'

Callery had been outside, where he'd taken a few deep breaths and tried to smell ozone, but got only petrol. The boat's engines were rumbling and churning beneath him, iron sharks eager to surge. He came back in and walked all the way round the deck where most passengers were gathering, in seats close to the bar and the restaurant. Then he went down to the deck below where the shops were, prowled there a bit, then went back upstairs and sprawled in a chair. He wanted a beer but there was already a mass of people at the bar; let them get served and settled first. Callery had his back to the room but had clocked other passengers when he first came in. The usual lot of messy humanity – but not that hoity-toity woman he'd noticed in the waiting area. She'd looked as though she couldn't wait to be somewhere else. A couple of beers when the queue had thinned down, a smooth crossing and then a taxi to Calais – and that lunch.

The ferry departed and a sense of excitement went through the lounge like a fresh wind; on our way! On the deck below, Becky's shop opened with a flurry of spraying from her. The bar got busier and Lauren was already replenishing the fridge with beers and small bottles of white wine. Steve darted between people, shelves and the till, chatting ceaselessly.

'Lager, sir? Comin' up—'

'Now then madam, what can I do for you?'

'Champagne, ladies? Special occasion is it – oh, a birthday? Twenty-one eh? No? Oh come on, I'll 'ave to ask you for some identification, ha ha ha!'

Lauren felt sick. As soon as it all calmed down she was going to slink off outside for a fag. Dirty old git Steve Sprauncey could deal with all these customers himself, if he was so good at it.

The Club Lounge was busy too, but in a quieter, less-impressed way. Jeanne Torbet sipped her chilled Sancerre (adequate) and regarded her fellow passengers. She imagined that the keys to some very comfortable and expensive cars jangled in various pockets. Cars that would be speeding their occupants smoothly and easily to Montreuil or to Honfleur – or maybe straight to Paris. Ah, Paris… she would check into the George Cinq, unpack, rest a short while and then descend to the bar for a glass of very expensive champagne. And, if things all went to plan, get into conversation with another guest; male, middle-aged and alone. Just him and his millions.

Becky wasn't doing too well in her shop. People weren't interested in buying perfume or cosmetics when they would soon be in France and could buy Givenchy or Chanel on the products' home turf, especially when Duty Free didn't apply anymore. It might be different on the way back, when the frenzy to keep buying stuff could drive passengers to chuck the last of their euros at something – anything – that postponed the reality of just living with what they'd already got. That quick shag with Steve hadn't been too good either – okay, quick was understandable what with boarding going on at the time, but he'd only looked after himself and ignored her needs. And he was probably still at it, eyeing up any fanciable passengers, giving them the same spiel he'd given her. That wasn't what Becky called a sincere relationship; if he carried on like that she'd break off their engagement which was a bit complicated anyway, what with him being still married with five kids. Becky decided she was being used. Then she decided to do fifteen per cent off lipsticks.

People wandered but some walked with a purpose. One of the passengers lurked…

****

'You finished with this?'

Orlando Fisham, Head of Art at Stuttenden school, looked up from his desk. His alcohol-bleared eyes met the reptilian ones of Sandra Moxey, the school's kitchen manageress.

'I beg your pardon, Mrs Moxey?'

Sandra nodded her head at the cup and saucer by Fisham's slightly shaking left hand. 'That. You finished with that there cup o' tea?'

Orlando gave her the china and tried to stop it rattling. 'Yes thank you.'

Sandra sneered. 'Feelin' bad? You should – you didn't 'alf have a skinful last night. That won't do you no good with the 'ead come salary reviews, will it?'

'Mind your own business. What are you doing up here anyway? You don't collect tea things.'

'No I bloody don't,' said Moxey bitterly. 'The bloody woman who usually does is off with bellyache or something, so Makepeace asked me ever so sweetly to help out. Cow. Still, it's a job – and you might not 'ave yours much longer.'

Orlando groaned. 'Go away, you odious old bag.'

Now Sandra laughed. 'I'll go away all right. An' so will you be goin' away come the end of this term, you see if you don't.' She shuffled off with her loaded tray. Orlando Fisham was appalled, yet again, at the woman's accent and pronunciation. He watched Sandra's broad backside push the door of his classroom open and then one foot pull it to as she went out. She was right, of course; he had got outrageously drunk at Jeanne Torbet's leaving dinner the evening before – and he probably had ruined his chances of a rise, maybe even of keeping his job. No, that was safe, he reckoned. But only because he was sleeping with Anishka Perry. He'd better do a bit of extra work in that direction tonight.

Sandra Moxey went back into her domain, the main kitchen at Stutters. She felt good there, powerful and safe. She knew about cooking on a large scale, she was comfortable with telling all the other women what to do. Head of Catering Logistics, that's what she was – fancy name for chief dinner lady. But she'd rather have been Nutrition Executive – that was what actually being in charge of all the food for the whole school meant. And *that* post was held by Lucy Makepeace. A smart, pretty, capable thirty-year-old on a huge salary and with the right to tell Sandra what to do. Lucy didn't interfere much in the kitchen – that's why Sandra felt at home there – but she was definitely the boss in her own office. And Sandra was called into that office several times a day. Little cow. Sandra Moxey pretended to admire and respect Lucy Makepeace, but privately she hated her. There was quite a lot of hate at Stuttenden.

****

The ferry had been at sea for about thirty minutes when a cleaner went into the women's toilets in the Club Lounge to do the usual checks – after checking that they were empty. She was surprised to find a hand-written notice stuck clumsily to the door of one of the cubicles: OUT OF ORDER. Funny, it hadn't been there when she'd cleaned the toilets before sailing – and nobody had informed her about a problem – and who'd written that note, anyway?

She pushed warily at the door; it wasn't locked but it almost immediately wedged up against something.

'You are there, somebody?' the cleaner called out. She hoped it wasn't a druggie who'd collapsed. She pushed a bit more and could now get a glimpse of who was inside. And then she screamed, loudly. Must get out, she thought, must get out this second, find Chief Steward, get away in case killer is still here—

Because a killer had been there. And now Jeanne Torbet's body lay slumped across the toilet seat, eyes bulging and tongue lolling from her mouth.

Chapter Two

Callery felt sick. Not with hunger, not with fear but with dread of what he knew was going to happen. Something bad had taken place on this ship, something bad and not normal; the law would have to be involved and he was The Law. Even though he was off-duty – no, not just off-duty, he was on holiday for god's sake, at this exact moment he was not a policeman, he was just a passenger on this boat to Calais, somebody wanting to get somewhere for a good time – he would have to own up and tell the captain of this bloody ship thing that he was a representative of Her Majesty's government and therefore able (no, probably obliged) to take control of the situation. Shit.

The ferry executed a graceful turn in the water and glided back to Dover. The announcement had caused a kind of suppressed uproar amongst the passengers; they knew that something dramatic must have happened but that it wasn't mechanical – the boat was moving as smoothly as if it was on ice. Somebody must have been taken ill, very very ill. Or had a terrorist been discovered on board? The suppression weakened a bit and some people started to look and sound panicky. But then another announcement was suddenly made; free drinks for all as an apology for the enormous inconvenience they were being caused, another vessel would be waiting as soon as the port was reached but in the meantime – a rush at the bar was immediate.

Aghast, Callery felt himself slip into the familiar mode of behaviour; go to the scene of the crime, talk to the person in charge, get a full list of people in the immediate vicinity, brief his sergeant and start on the long, long, careful haul of enquiries. He met the DS who'd come on board to assist, hastily recruited from the nearest station to the port. The body was boring because predictable in its ghastliness, quickly dealt with before being handed on to the pathologist, also local and hastily called upon.

The passengers' initial stupor of shock at being brought back to Dover was quickly turning to impatience as the novelty of free drinks wore off. Mutterings about official complaints, refunds and then the dreaded word compensation began to circulate. The captain carried on being co-operative but looked agitated. Callery and the DS got enough details and photocopies of passports to be going on with and the boat was emptied in only a few hours, but it seemed to everybody like an eternity. Callery missed Peattie.

The boat was a boat again, not a crime scene. It waited for passengers to reboard. The body had gone, forensics had finished, all the information that could be gleaned initially had been gathered, recorded. Callery had all he needed to start the proper enquiry. He knew the name of the victim and her last address; Jeanne Torbet, until yesterday a language teacher at Stuttenden school in Kent. He was now off to an affluent private educational establishment forty miles inland – and not sitting in a slightly shabby but charming little restaurant in Calais. He wouldn't be eating a huge bowl of moules followed by steak frites; Callery would be lucky if he managed to stuff in a few packs of sandwiches from a service station on the way to the school. As the police car left the port he stared rigidly at Dover castle and kept the coast of France behind him; he couldn't bear to look.

It got worse; he rang his Superintendent and was told that because of huge cuts the police force had had to make in recent months, not only would Callery not have a team to investigate with, he wouldn't even have a sergeant to assist him. Callery wouldn't have had his old one anyway; Peattie had moved on. But this - this meant You're On Your Own, Chum. Nonsense, the Super said when Callery protested, you will have a team back at base – shared with other investigations of course, but available twenty-four seven by text, phone and email. All back up – liaising with forensics, secondary enquiries, collating reports – would be dealt with in-house. Callery wouldn't be understaffed, he'd be free to use his unique skills in immersing himself in the school in order to find the killer. Yeah, thought Callery, I bet these cuts haven't taken a penny out of your personal expenses budget, sir.

****

Anishka Perry was annoyed. Extremely annoyed. To be called out of any meeting with governors present was highly unacceptable, but to be told – *told,* not asked – to leave people who had literally millions to give to the school, millions that she could charm from them with the utmost integrity – that was outrageous. 'Tell whoever it is I can't, I'm busy,' Perry instructed her PA, whispering fiercely into her phone while the governors advised the prospective investors where to have lunch after the meeting.

'He insists,' said the PA. Lou Shelbourne was prepared to be shouted at by her boss – it happened on average four times a day, followed by a gushing apology and insincere hug – but she knew when to stand her ground. And a six foot god-knows-how-much policeman with a pissed off look on his face was, she reckoned, more than a match for Perry in stubbornness, if not arrogance.

'Who is he? If he's not a billionaire desperate to chuck a fortune my way then I won't see him.'

'He's the police. Something very serious has happened, he says.'

'Oh for god's— okay, I'm coming out.'

Perry grovelled apologies to the meeting and stalked into her office to meet this bloody policeman, whoever he was; her five foot one teetering on four-inch heels. And for what? Some stupid misdemeanour on the part of a pupil, probably; one of the truly rich, utterly spoiled ones. Anishka sighed. This sort of thing wasn't what a future Prime Minister should have to deal with. She led her stellar career's intruder into her office and closed the door. Outside, Lou Shelbourne speculated wildly.

'Ms Anishka Perry, head of Stuttenden school?'

The ridiculously tall, thin and very unattractive man standing in there seemed to have the idea that he could demand information from her. That hadn't happened since she was three years old. Anishka Perry had jettisoned two adoring but backward parents, one husband and anyone who had helped her in the past but was of no use to her now – and she didn't intend to stay as Head at Stuttenden for life. She was going to be the first ever Asian female leader of a Conservative government and nothing was going to get in her way.

'I am,' she replied haughtily.

Callery flashed his identification card at her.

'And you have a member of staff by the name of Jeanne Torbet?'

'I had. She was our French teacher, but left the school yesterday.'

'I'm afraid to tell you that she has been killed.'

The haughtiness dissolved into shock. '*Killed?* How?'

'She was found dead on a cross channel ferry earlier today,' said Callery in a blank tone of voice. 'Strangled.'

'But this is awful. Appalling.' Anishka Perry dropped into the chair at her desk. 'She— she was here yesterday; she— she'd resigned. She was going back to France, apparently.'

'Can you think of anyone who might have had a motive for her murder?' Callery looked at Anishka as if he expected her to say *yes you're quite right, me.* She shook her head.

'Nobody else on your staff had any reason to hate her?'

'No. She wasn't exactly popular – she was too aloof for that – but nobody here had the sort of grudge that would drive them to do that.'

'How do you know? Can you know everything about the relationships between your teachers, Ms Perry?'

The haughtiness came back. 'I don't allow personal connections in my school.'

'But you couldn't prevent them, could you – and if anything like that was kept secret you wouldn't know, would you?'

'Well of course not, if they were really sneaky about it – but I just told you, Ms Torbet wasn't friendly enough with anybody. There— there was a gulf between her and the others. A gulf she created herself.'

'Was she aloof with her pupils?'

Perry laughed at that. 'Oh with *some* of them she was the exact opposite! Cliquey; she seemed to like a little group hovering around— or rather she wanted them to adore *her.*'

'Did you like Jeanne Torbet?'

'Not much. But she was an excellent teacher. I always treated her with a distanced respect.'

Callery grunted. 'Okay. Now, I'm afraid I'm going to have to ask you to do something that will be difficult and unpleasant, Ms Perry.'

'Oh god, you don't mean I've got to identify the body?'

'Yes.'

Anishka sighed unhappily. The road to Number 10 was full of challenges; she had to be prepared for actions like this.

'Okay. Now?'

'Yes please. The sooner our enquiries can proceed the better, I'm sure you can understand that.'

'Of course.'

****

Identification took place and was swift and decisive; the body was that of Jeanne Torbet. Callery found a room above the village pub, a comfortable-looking place called The Haunted Chimney. Here we go again, he thought, me over a pub in a village dealing with a murder. He plunged into enquiries with a definite purpose now; somebody – possibly, probably from the school where she had taught – had followed Torbet onto the boat and strangled her. Callery set up his laptop, then went downstairs to the bar for some food.

Once he'd got himself on the outside of a vast portion of ale pie and chips (not bad) and a couple of pints of the pub's own brew (even more not bad) he made a list of Where To Start. The first thing was to speak to everybody who worked at the school; teachers, employees in the building who didn't teach (Callery had quickly learned from the Head to call them support staff), the gardeners (he just as quickly learnt to call *them* ancillary staff). A lot of people. He hoped it would be a pretty straightforward process to slice it down to anyone who'd had a genuine connection to Jeanne Torbet. Perry had said that only a few of the teachers, one support staff manager, her main team member and the only gardener who was on-site full time would have had any contact with Jeanne Torbet. All the rest had never had any connection with her, didn't know her. From hundreds the suspects could be just a manageable nine, brilliant. Aniska Perry herself, the headmistress. The four other language teachers and the head of art, all of whom were apparently in something that had to be called the Expression Pod. *Expression Pod?* Jesus, whatever happened to classrooms, Callery thought. It was probably totally wrong of him to think of Perry as the headmistress; she would make him refer to her as the Knowledge Enabler or something. Then there was Lucy Makepeace, who was in charge of catering and Sandra Moxey, who actually ran the kitchens. And Adam Thicklow, who kept the fancy flower beds and immaculate lawns in shape.

Callery bought another pint and looked round the pub, something else that helped Where To Start. Wealth, confidence, pleasure, everywhere. The pub's clientele were almost uniformly in their thirties to fifties, healthy, good-looking and well-dressed and totally at ease with everything. Life suited them; they didn't have to suit it. They might have had to at some earlier point – Callery could well imagine the older men especially having started from unprivileged circumstances – but now success had been strived for, grabbed and tamed. There were no women in their fifties crowding the bar or seated in the stylish easy chairs by the stylish woodburner. Callery noticed that the women were demonstrably younger all round, some of them in their thirties and the ones clinging to the older men surely not beyond thirty itself. And the teeth! Because everybody was having such a good time, drinking and laughing, immaculate molars sparkled everywhere. So did cared-for nails, skin – even the men obviously had regular manicures. Callery felt like a bit of manure wrongly left on show at the Chelsea Flower Show. Okay, this village was bursting with money and certainty, this was good to know. This village was sort of immune to ordinary life. Yeah, but this village had a murder in its midst, he'd got to find out who'd done it and he would. The bit of manure caught the eye of the young man clearing glasses and ordered another pint.

Chapter Three

Callery got properly going the next day. He went to the school and started off by talking to somebody who presumably had the best overview of life there, Perry's PA. He knocked on her door and her friendly voice told him to come in, so he did.

'Ms...' – more checking of names on his list – 'Shelbourne, thank you for introducing me to your boss yesterday. Could we have a brief chat?'

'The Head isn't here,' said Lou with a wary look.

'Not her; you.'

'Of course,' said Lou. Hooray, she thought, more information and this time from the source. Anishka Perry had told her about the appalling thing that had happened to a member of staff, but nothing more.

This woman seemed very nice and it rubbed off on Callery. Bit of small talk first, don't plunge in with disturbing facts and questions straightaway.

'Ms Lou Shelbourne, yes. I suppose Lou is short for Louise?'

'No, it's just Lou, always has been. It's where I was conceived.'

Callery stared. 'Right – er, yes. Er, tell me what you thought of Jeanne Torbet; did you have much contact with her? Ms Perry intimated that she wasn't very popular.'

'Oh I see teachers all the time,' said Lou Shelbourne, smiling. 'They pop in to complain to the head about each other, or try and get some tasty bits of gossip from me. I'm not sure why; I'm stuck in here all day, so I'm the last person to hear any tittle-tattle. And Ms Perry is very insistent that I keep all but the most important issues from her. Jeanne, hmm, well the impression I got was that she was rather standoffish – didn't join in, didn't gel with the school or anyone in it.'

'She didn't ever open up to you at all, as a non-teacher – maybe she felt intimidated amongst the rest of the staff; foreign, on her own? She was unmarried, in a strange country?'

'Yes, that's true. But no, she never came in here except for anything to do with practical matters – you know, her contract, teaching hours, class numbers. I don't know – I got the feeling from the other language teachers that she was just cold, she wanted to be unapproachable.'

'And Ms Perry; she's a good person to work for?'

Lou was always keen to chat about personalities, but she was still loyal. 'How exactly is that connected with the murder?'

'Anything about anybody at this school is going to help me build up a picture of the place where a murderer evolved,' Callery said, shrugging.

Lou didn't shrug, she shuddered. 'Don't, that really brings it home, literally – you mean somebody here actually planned and killed Jeanne Torbet?'

'It's a strong initial theory I'm working on.'

'Isn't there usually two of you? You know, a lead detective and their – sergeant, isn't it? You know, Morse and Lewis, then Lewis and Hathaway? My parents love those old programmes, they watch them all the time.'

Callery felt like unburdening himself to this nice, open woman, telling her how he'd been dumped with this enquiry without any real support whatsoever. But he, too, had a residual loyalty. Plus he was embarrassed, bloody Super. He mumbled something about slashed budgets and streamlined practices, said thankyou and left. He needed to speak to everybody else who worked at the school; teachers, other employees in the building who didn't teach and the gardeners.

Three of the remaining language teachers were soon eliminated; Sylvia Bianchi, who taught Italian and Greek, had been away on a course to learn Mandarin Chinese. Blimey. Beatriz Abreu, who taught Portuguese and Spanish was absent because she was giving birth to triplets. Blimey again. Hanna Fischer, in charge of German, was on compassionate leave at home in Berlin after a family bereavement. All easily confirmed, as were the alibis for all the other teachers in all the other departments. So were those of most of the kitchen workers and cleaners. Callery hated admitting it – the challenge of any crime should be almost relished, he'd been trained that way – but it did make his job easier. The only language teacher who needed to be kept in sight was Everard Hayes, Head of English. And the only non-language teacher who taught in close vicinity to Jeanne Torbet was somebody called Orlando Fisham, Head of Art.

****

Fisham had just finished his last lesson of the day and it was still only five to three. He went to his study and poured himself a large whisky. There wasn't too much danger of anybody important walking in on him; Perry was in a governors' meeting until at least five o'clock, sucking up to a possible sponsor for the new concert hall. Orlando took a good swig, glanced out of the window then nearly spurted it all out again. As he'd taken the ever-helpful amber liquid into his mouth he'd spotted a police car whizzing up the drive. Christ; those fake carer's claims, had he been rumbled already? He swallowed the whisky pleasurelessly, shoved the glass and bottle back into the bottom drawer of his desk and looked for something to get rid of the smell on his breath. The cleaner usually left stuff after cleaning the cloakroom that his office shared with Torbet. Fisham darted in there and grabbed the first aerosol he saw without turning on the light. Spraying products didn't usually contain bleach, right? He aimed a quick squirt into his open mouth and the most nauseating taste of chemical honeysuckle hit his tongue. He thought about another quick swallow of whisky but then there was a sharp knock at the door; they were here.

It wasn't a They though, just one tall policeman. Callery glowered at Fisham. He always started with a glower with men; it made them pay attention to his questions.

'Mr. Orlando Fisham?'

Orlando sat down under the glower and nodded, then coughed.

'You are, er, Head of the Art Department at this school?'

It wasn't a good idea to clear one's throat to answer a question shortly after imbibing air freshener. A rush of spray forced itself back into his mouth and he retched.

'*Eeurgh! Argh*! Sorry, so sorry, bit of a throat – yes, yes that's correct.'

Callery stared impassively at Orlando. 'Funny smell for cough mixture. How well did you know Jeanne Torbet?'

'Er well, you know, well enough in a professional capacity, but not well otherwise – I mean, we never met outside of school hours – and I only really saw her if we passed in the corridors or if we entered or left our offices at the same time.' God, the taste of whisky-tainted bog perfume was vile.

'What did you think of her?'

'I— she— I didn't really have much of an opinion. She was good at her job, I think. French and Art don't really coincide much as subjects.'

'Apart from French artists.'

'Eh? Oh, yes – ha ha, of course, Monet, Renoir, Cezanne et al. Very good.' Fisham gave a queasy smile.

'Well, that will be all for now, thankyou sir.' Callery left. Orlando retched again and delved for the bottle of whisky.

****

It was only a civil knock, but Everard Hayes reacted as if Callery had bludgeoned through the door like a human axe.

'Yes! What! Come – come in, give me a moment—'

Callery went in. Hayes was sitting at his desk; his clothing was dishevelled and so was his breathing. It was a small room – surely nobody could get up to anything to make them look so desperate in a confined, cluttered space like this? Or had that itself caused the ruffled response? Hayes seemed as unnerved as Fisham; what was the matter with this place?

'Mr Hayes? A word, if you don't mind?' Callery flashed his card. Everard Hayes' glassy-eyed look didn't even catch it. 'Yes?' he gulped again.

'You are Everard Hayes, Head of English at this school?'

'I am.' Hayes looked as if teaching English was tantamount to being a Nazi.

'It's about the murder of Jeanne Torbet. Your fellow teacher at this school.'

'Oh god yes.' The glassy, sweating demeanour dropped away and Hayes started looking like somebody who, whatever he got up to, it hadn't been anything as bad as bumping somebody else off.

The interview didn't last long and went smoothly from then on; Hayes hadn't known Torbet well, knew nothing of her private life, had no idea who might have killed her. Of course he would let Callery know if he thought of anything else that could help the investigation. Yeah yeah yeah – Callery was getting fed up with these people at this school; they all seemed to be making it obvious that they had something to hide yet knew bugger all about anything else, especially Jeanne Torbet's life and death.

****

Callery wanted some fresh air, so he went outside and in search of Adam Thicklow, the gardener. He found him behind the main building and almost at the edge of the school grounds.

'Could I have a word, Mr. Thicklow?'

The tall, handsome young man stretched up from doing whatever gardeners did with flower beds and faced Callery, smiled hesitantly and then looked serious.

'Course.' Adam Thicklow rubbed earth from his hands and shoved them into the pockets of a scruffy but somehow elegant tweed jacket.

'You are the head gardener here at this school?'

'Yep. Well no. Not Head, Executive. Executive Agricultural Administrator, that's the official thing they call me, my official job.' A self-deprecating grin slipped over his face.

'You've heard about the death – the killing – of Jeanne Torbet, a teacher at this school?'

'Yeah, terrible that.'

'How much contact did you have with the deceased?'.

A shrug. 'Well, none really. I'm just a gardener here, she was a teacher.'

'A good one?'

Another shrug, hands still stylishly in those pockets. 'I think so, dunno really. As I say, I'm always out here and— and she was always in there.' He nodded towards the glorious Gothic mansion that was the face of Stuttenden school; the beautiful, enticing Victorian front of a very controlled, successful, money-driven and modern business.

'But you came across her at some point?'

'Not really, no not ever – apart from the end of term parties, Anishka – Ms Perry – was always very keen that we all went to those.'

'You met Ms Torbet at one of these parties then?'

'She was getting a glass of wine from the free bar when I was asking for a beer, that's all. She looked at me, I smiled and – and she didn't. That was it.'

'No conversation?'

Thicklow laughed quietly. 'According to the girls their French teacher didn't think it was worth talking to anybody who wasn't going to do anything for her career.'

'The girls? You mean the pupils, the ones Torbet taught?'

'Uh-huh.'

'Have much to do with the girls, do you Mr Thicklow?' Callery's real version of the question was: do you screw the pupils?

'Not really – look, as I said, I'm out here, I've got nothing to do with what goes on in there. I see some of the students if they come out into the grounds, okay? I think they like to wind me up, make me think they fancy me.'

'Maybe some of them do; you're not a bad-looking bloke.'

Thicklow blushed. 'I'm not interested in children, Inspector.'

Callery let Thicklow get back to work. As he walked away he wondered exactly who Adam Thicklow *was* interested in – or more to the point really, who was interested in him?

****

And then it was as if a heavy black cloud had suddenly been plucked away from the sky over Stuttenden – Callery met somebody who wasn't wary or downright scared but direct, open and cheerful. He was shown into the office of Lucy Makepeace.

'I'm so sorry I wasn't here when you started your enquiries, Detective Inspector; I was at a conference in Manchester. You were told?' Ms Makepeace's smile was natural and delightful; she was slim, blonde and not very tall.

'It was explained to me, yes.' Callery felt as if he was back outside, in a garden full of sunshine, spring flowers and birdsong instead of a small, file-cluttered room.

'Please, take a seat.' Ms Makepeace sat down herself and replaced the lovely smile with an equally-charming look of concern. 'This is a terrible thing to have happened – to Jeanne, such a good teacher and respected colleague.'

Callery shot her a glance. 'You liked Ms Torbet?'

'Well, our paths didn't really cross enough for us to have a *liking* sort of connection, but we— we never had any arguments or anything. She was a bit— well, a bit standoffish, I suppose. Not a mixer.'

'She had quite a close band of pupils, apparently. Mixed with them.'

Makepeace looked suspicious – here we go, thought Callery, somebody else pulling the blind down on me, more wariness and guile.

'What do you mean?'

'Oh nothing really,' said Callery blithely. 'Just that I heard she had this little group of the students she taught who were… very loyal. The word clique was used.'

'Who by? Was it Sandra Moxey?'

Callery looked briefly at his notes. 'Ah – she's Head Cook. Under you.'

'Yes, she's a member of my staff. She—' Lucy Makepeace gave a weary sigh. 'She's rather difficult to work with.'

'In what way?'

'Oh, resistant to new concepts, sadly lacking in interpersonal skills.' Then the warm smile came back. 'If Ms Torbet inspired commitment in her classes that was a good thing, surely?'

'You are overall Head of Catering at this school, yes?'

There was a very slight wince behind the ready smile. 'Far more than that. My official title is Nutrition Director. I curate the dining experience for our pupils.' Makepeace was smiling but serious; Callery thought she should be laughing after saying something like that.

'But that means you have the final say, surely?'

The smile widened. 'Oh I have every say, Inspector Callery. It's just that… Sandra hates me.' Lucy Makepeace looked down at a sheet of paper on her desk and frowned. 'I do so want everybody who works for me to feel a sense of achievement.' She sighed, then looked back up with the radiant smile splashed on again.

'You must try one of our lunches sometime. Why not tomorrow?'

Callery demurred. 'I wouldn't want to get in the way—'

'You won't.' Makepeace clicked at her computer and glanced at the screen. 'Chicken chasseur or a vegan alternative, salads with sourdough ciabatta followed by pear strudel or fresh fruit. Does any of that tempt you?'

Callery nearly drooled. 'What time shall I come to the canteen?'

'The refectory, Inspector. There is no canteen at Stuttenden. Come at midday, before our lively students descend.'

****

Callery left Lucy Makepeace's office and went into the actual kitchens to speak to Sandra Moxey herself. He thought he'd like her; a cook, solid and sensible with no paranoia about her place in the teaching hierarchy, just a normal person to talk to. Charming and co-operative as Makepeace had been, even she had shown her ambition. But Moxey was ghastly, right from the start.

'Your name is—?' Callery didn't get to finish his opening question.

'My professional or private one?' Callery was being given a stare that would intimidate a rampaging bear.

'Er, both?'

'I goes by the Moxey one here but that's my work name, okay? Sandra Moxey. But in real actual life I'm Magdalen Yvonne Olivia Betty. All right?'

'That's quite a mouthful.'

'Swallow it.'

Callery took a breath. 'Magdalen and all those others Moxey?'

'You can have that or nothing else.'

'I'm sorry, Ms Moxey,' – Callery wasn't sorry, ever – 'but why are you so hostile?'

'Why are you here?'

'I'm investigating a murder. You must know that.'

'Yeah, but I don't know who did it, do I? So you're wastin' your time – and time to me is money, I 'ave to do my job in this school, so if you'll just sod off and let me do it—'

'Ms Moxey, if you don't co-operate then I will take you to the nearest police station for questioning on a formal, possibly cautioned basis. *Or you*—'

Sandra Moxey raised her thick, strangely-threatening eyebrows. 'Or what – I could be charged with obstructing bollocks – oh all right, *here's* what I'll tell you and that's all I'll tell you and that's all that'll be of any bloody use. *Okay?*'

Callery knew when to be flexible. 'Okay.'

'Right. That Torbet was a cow, through and through. Taught all right but was a snotty bitch with everybody except her tight little circle – and even then she wasn't that sweet – she was a cold French snotty cow and nobody liked her. All the other teachers are useless twits or drunks or perverts or all of them things and I wouldn't let one of my kids anywhere near 'em – and all those poncey thievin' bastard parents actually *pay* for that to happen!'

Sandra Moxey stopped speaking and Callery processed what had been flung at him. This woman was a good witness – not to definite events, but to the whole world that was Stuttenden school. She was invaluable – and unbearable.

'You seem to have a very perceptive view of the staff here. I wouldn't mind your thoughts on another couple of members – Mr Hayes? Adam Thicklow, the gardener?'

Sandra Moxey almost foamed at the mouth. 'Thicklow? Him? I could tell you stuff about *him*.'

'Go ahead, tell us.'

'Brain in his trousers. All sorts, all the time. 'E's got hisself into the right person's pants, I know that for a fact. I know lots against folk 'ere.'

Callery logged this for later. 'And Mr Hayes?'

'Well now he'd *like* to be as active as bloody Thicklow, but he can't.'

'Can't what, exactly?'

'Can't do nothing – can't have the sex he wants, can't teach – the kids treat 'im like a joke – can't get on with Perry so's she'll make him feel more important. But avin' said that, e's not a total arse-licker like most of 'em are – he does question what Ms I'm Goin' Places Perry says sometimes.'

'Yes, Ms Perry; what is your opinion of her?' Callery suspected what was coming.

'Crafty, fakin' it all the time,' Sandra Moxey said with a shrug. Then she leaned close to Callery and jabbed at him with a meaty finger. 'She's up to all sorts and that's a fact.'

'Is that likely? She's in a responsible position,' said Callery. 'I mean, if she jeopardised that in any way with her employers she could – well, seriously fall out of favour.'

'I wish she'd fall out of a plane.'

'Do you like anybody, Ms Moxey?'

There was a pause; Callery waited to see what Sandra Moxey said. The other catering staff? *Any* of the pupils?

'I like the person who puts my wages in my bank account every month.'

'Right. Well, I think that's all… for now.' Callery tried to make those last two words sound ominous – but Moxey beat him to it.

'You bet it is, copper.'

Callery told himself he'd had enough for one day. As with the other four, he took an official statement from Sandra Moxey (as quickly as possible, with her) and went back to the pub.

Chapter Four

The next morning Callery stayed in his room at The Haunted Chimney, recording his progress on the case, which was not much. Then he went out and walked round the village before going into the corner shop. It wasn't the usual sort – of course not, thought Callery, this is Stuttenden, nothing's usual here. It didn't have not-very-good quality food, cheap wine and a vast range of bagged snacks and chemical-laden sweets. Oh no. Poynters sold what looked to Callery like top-notch fruit and veg, had an excellent wine section and the cheapest bag of crisps seemed to be an oven-baked root vegetable combination called Shredz, priced at two pounds. Callery waited until the pleasant-looking woman at the cash desk finished with a customer and spoke to her, flashing his card.

'It's about the murder, isn't it' she said, smiling excitedly. 'I mean, fancy us having a murder here in our village, it's too posh for that!'

'Could you tell me who you are?' asked Callery, refusing to smile back.

'Me? I'm Lisa Choke; I'm the manageress here.'

'Do you own this shop?'

'I wish!' The wide grin, which had momentarily dropped at Callery's lack of one, whipped back. 'That would be Marcus Hedding – he owns the estate agent a bit further up—' Lisa Choke gestured backwards with her head. Callery presumed she meant further along the road outside, where a couple more shops paved the way to the church.

'Why is it called Poynters then?'

'That was Marcus's mum's maiden name; her family started the shop in the nineteenth century. It's the oldest shop in the county!' Lisa said proudly.

'Oh really,' said Callery, unimpressed. Being near all this food was making him hungry.

'Very wealthy family, the Poynters. And Marcus's mother, she brought a lot of it with her when she married Marcus's dad and then inherited the rest of it when he died. Some people have all the luck, eh!'

'I suppose you get many of the pupils at the school in here,' said Callery, trying not to look at some pasties and sausage rolls that were lazing in the heat of a glass-fronted oven by the counter. 'Teachers, too – Jeanne Torbet, for instance, the French teacher?'

'The murder victim!' Lisa declaimed. 'Well no, not really. I heard some of the other teachers talk about her though.' Lisa bent forward and lowered her voice. 'They didn't like her.'

'What did they say?'

'Stuff about her being stuck-up and not joining in anything. They were discussing a walk they were all planning on doing – for charity, it was – and one of them said that this Ms Torbet had refused to take part, and then another of 'em said well that's just typical of her, isn't it, she don't want to do anything with the likes of us.'

'So you never met the woman herself?'

'No. Shame – we stock a lovely Brie.'

Just then the door was flung open and a horde of schoolkids burst in, shouting and screaming. Lisa Choke looked at Callery and shouted too.

'I'm sorry, I'll have to deal with this lot now, can't talk anymore – hey!' She barged out from behind the counter and – incredibly for a small woman – took control of a hustling crowd of gangly, famished teens. Callery ducked out of the shop and to Stutters.

After talking to a nice, ordinary woman like Ms Choke, Callery felt he could face more negativity. He decided to interview – in a casual, roundabout way – some of the pupils, especially the girls in Jeanne Torbet's supposed special group. He decided on them first; they were in what had been Torbet's office, lounging in chairs placed around her desk as if they expected her to walk in at any moment, when they would sit up and look adoring. Six unreasonably glamorous faces turned confidently towards him. Confident, but slightly contemptuous too. They didn't look anything like the girls Callery had been at school with; they were more like women acting in a film about schoolgirls. He started off trying to be egalitarian, show he was in touch with everybody in the school and not just the teaching staff – the management. Hence an opening chat about who he'd spoken to already at Stutters.

'*Who?*' said one of them, her fearsomely sculpted eyebrows raised in patrician query. The others sniggered.

'Magdalen Yvonne Olivia Betty – that's Ms Moxey's full names,' said Callery, knowing he was going to be the twit out of this.

Eyebrows joined the rest of the backing group in the laughing chorus behind Callery's daft question.

'What?' he asked. 'That's not her real name— names?'

'Are you kidding?' said one.

'She's *Sandra*,' said another.

'She's just a cook,' said a third, still giggling. 'Cooks don't have names like that.'

'Right,' said Callery, completely in the wrong. 'Not Magdalen and all those other—'

One of the girls laughed in a kinder way. 'No, she's having you on! Those names she gave you, the initials – don't you get it?'

Callery computed. 'M, Y, O, B – oh.' He laughed too now, but lamely. 'Mind Your— yeah, got it.'

'Pathetic, but Sandra Moxey's idea of wit,' said the kind girl.

'She's horrible; she hates us and we hate her,' said another.

This gave Callery a way back in to a proper conversation. 'But you all liked Ms Torbet?'

There was a chorus again – but not laughing this time, just aahs of approbation.

'She was *great*,' said a big girl wearing what looked like three pairs of false eyelashes. 'She really enabled us to connect to the Lingual Other, to like, start on our journeys to a different wordscape from the ones we were, you know, birthed into in the patriarchal speakworld that my mother says is all women's plight from the moment of their, like, conception.'

'Oh shut up Chloe,' said the kind girl, but not in a kind way. 'Torbet taught us French and she was brilliant at it and she understood that we were special so she took us to Paris that fabulous week and that's all. And your mum's mad.'

That got more laughter. Chloe started batting the eyelashes; Callery thought if she does that long enough she'll take off.

'Paris? When was that? What did you do?'

There was a collected huff, as if he should have known. Then another girl piped up; this one seemed to have lips that heaved at Callery as much as her surely-not-her-age breasts did. He started to feel vulnerable, like a six-year-old who'd come across his older sisters' very worldly mates.

'You want an itinerary? My father's PA has the exacts records if you need them, but we can remember—' she looked around for the confirmation she knew she'd get. 'Okay, yeah, Eurostar from London on the Friday, check-in at Manon's stepmother's apartment before we all shopped like crazy, then dinner with Madame Torbet and the culture secretary at the George Cinq – he's one of Manon's ex-husbands – *so* boring, then—' Lips giggled, looked at the others and they all laughed in support.

'Then,' said yet another one of these frightening pre-women. 'Then we escaped and went to enjoy the *real* Paris.' More laughter, like satisfied courtesans who knew they ruled a country.

'Where?' Was Madame Torbet with you by now?' Callery asked. Please don't tell me she was in charge of all this, he thought.

'Of course not – she was a great teacher, we adored her, but that was all – who'd want her around in Paris on a Friday evening?'

A small girl who wasn't like the rest; no enhanced brows or lips or, god forbid, breasts had spoken. Callery thought ah, maybe this was the sort of shy, entranced pupil he could get to, one who'd help him understand the hold Torbet had over her students.

'But she'd have liked you to be with her?'

The small girl stared. 'Fuck that, she got us to Paris and as far as we were concerned that was all we needed her for.' She turned to the others. 'When did we all get back to that fucking boring apartment? God, all that *service,* all the fucking time—'

The others chorused. 'In time for breakfast!'

'Oh yes,' said Chloe. 'Croissants et confiture avec café servi par les jeunes hommes très *très* gentils!' More clique laughter.

'Breakfast Saturday morning?' said Callery.

'*Naah!!!*' More shrieks. 'Monday of course!'

Yet another girl spoke up; this one looked as though she had four children and had been married to a cabinet minister for twenty years. Her voice was calm and mature, her tone measured and distinctly patronizing. 'We were very close to Torbet – and she to us – but she understood how much our parents would have wanted us to get the most out of a brief stay in such an amazing city. There was a – how shall I put it – a mutually appreciative laxity on both sides.'

Callery would have put it as spoiled bloody kids doing what they want and a teacher only too happy to let them do it, but told himself to shut up.

'Where do you think Madame Torbet spent the weekend then?' He asked, pointlessly.

'We didn't see her until the Monday – she just wanted to look in and see that we were okay – and then we were with her properly again on the last evening when we all had to gather and dine in some really fancy restaurant with – who was it, Shameless?'

The small swearing girl replied. 'Oh god yeah, the fucking president,' she said, drained of all interest.

'But. I'm sorry – you started off all saying how much you loved her, respected her. And now—'

'She *was* wonderful, always,' said Chloe, eyelashes landing safely. 'That was why we loved her, the fact that she let us experience Paris in the way we wanted, she trusted us and left us alone.' She blinked and two huge tears dropped onto her cheeks as if the astounding lashes had swept them there.

****

Callery went back to his room, depressed. Those girls were frightening in their superiority, the way their privilege had made them take a short cut from childhood to complete cynicism. He had a quick sleep, then went downstairs to eat. He decided to stay downstairs and hoped that one or other of the teachers would come in; after twenty minutes or so, Everard Hayes did.

He stood a bit along the bar from Callery, but close enough to be heard ordering a triple brandy, with another quite soon when you're ready dear child. Callery waited for him to get nearer; he did.

'Good evening Inspector!' The forced jollity was palpable. 'Off-duty, I see—' Hayes nodded towards the pint glass in Callery's fist. It was nearly empty, but that and the off-duty acknowledgement didn't prompt Hayes to ask if he'd like another. Callery muttered a yes.

'Are your enquiries – if I may ask – proceeding well?' The triple brandy had gone and the pre-ordered second one had arrived. That made six.

'I'm— we're making progress,' Callery said non-commitally.

'Any suspects specifically in mind?' The question was put casually, but Callery sensed the worry behind it.

'Plenty.'

Hayes gulped at his brandy as if it was the branch of a eucalyptus tree and he was a starving koala. Callery decided to let him off the hook.

'But suspects aren't criminals, not until they're charged – then they stop being suspects and become felons.'

'Right,' said Hayes, taking another but more relaxed swallow. 'Of course. Shouldn't ask really I suppose, you being here in a social context and not a professional one.'

Callery grunted, then motioned to the barmaid for another pint. Off-duty or not, he wasn't going to buy a ninth lot of brandy for Everard Hayes.

'You enjoy your job, Mr. Hayes?' he asked.

There was a significant pause, which the two men understood and appreciated. 'Not really.'

'I get the feeling,' Callery said, feeling his way. 'That nobody really likes working at Stuttenden – you all seem to be not quite at ease in your various positions. Why? It's an affluent, flourishing school in a wealthy, attractive village – what's the problem?'

Hayes took the last swig from his glass and signalled to the barmaid for another triple. He seemed to let something go, as if Callery's question had enabled him to truly relax and be honest.

'I don't know. It's not the Head – she's a hard-nosed bitch who doesn't give a stuff about children and education, she just wants to run the country – but it's not her. It's not any of us, as buggered-up as we all are, for various reasons. It isn't a lack of funding – you can see that, the school's rolling in money. But something's rotten in the state of Denmark. I hope you find out what it is.' The third triple arrived and Hayes did it justice.

'That's interesting Mr. Hayes,' said Callery. It was.

Hayes looked Callery straight in the eye – a first. 'I think – I think Ms Torbet was the absolute apogee of that rottenness. She somehow added to it and brought it to a head.'

'With her murder, you mean?'

'Yes. She sort of pushed the poison in this school to a peak – I don't know how – and then suffered from it.'

'That's even more interesting, Mr Hayes.'

'Is it? Then it's the first interesting thing I've said or thought for a long time.' Hayes took another last gulp from his glass.

Callery suddenly quite liked this man. Behind the terrified bluster and superciliousness was a sharper bloke than he'd at first thought. 'As I'm off-duty, this is allowed; would you like another drink?'

Chapter Five

Callery felt encouraged. He'd found a chink in the wall of distrust, dislike and condescension that he'd faced the first moment he'd set foot in Stuttenden – not the village itself so much, but the school. Everard Hayes wasn't an ally exactly, but he was an indication that the truth about Jeanne Torbet's death could be uncovered.

He started the following day with a renewed search for the truth from a liar.

'You gave me a false name, Ms Moxey.'

'So?' Sandra Moxey stood at the door of her office and glared at Callery, like somebody who was about to tell a cold caller to fuck off.

'I could interpret that as wasting police time.'

'Interpret what you like – I'm not the language teacher around here. We had one, didn't we? And she's dead.'

'Well anyway, that's not important – unless you lie about everything. Do you?'

'No. Which could be a fib itself, couldn't it Mr Smarty Arse?' Sandra Moxey smirked.

'Why do you hate me?'

'I hates everybody. I told you they're all bastards in this place – I do my job an' I keep away from everything else. *Everything.*' She gave a huge, breast-raising and lowering sigh.

'What does everything mean?'

Now it was one of her eyebrows' turn to be hoisted. 'Like I told you last time you bothered me, what goes on here. The people at it think they're gettin' away with it, right? But they won't get away with it for long.'

'Do you mean somebody's going to inform on them – to the authorities?'

Callery got the eyebrow treatment again.

'Anything else?' he asked.

Moxey dropped her ghastly, braying voice and looked at Callery meaningfully. 'Talk to one of the governors. Ask around for the one who owns a string of nightclubs in Spain.'

'What's he called?'

'Keith Hunt.'

Callery was surprised. He'd expected a nightlife entrepreneur to have a more glamorous name somehow, like Stringfellow or Rubin. And Moxey's outspokenness was catching.

'That's quite boring.'

'It's better than if his initials was the other way round.'

Callery wouldn't let himself laugh, although he wanted to.

'I'll follow up on your suggestion. Anything else you wish to tell me, Ms Moxey?'

'Cabbages.'

'Pardon?'

'Cabbages. I gotta get on the phone and order a whole load for tomorrow.'

'I'm not stopping you,' Callery said sourly – Moxey's bitterness was catching.

'No you ain't,' she spat at him. Sandra Moxey went over to her desk, thumped herself into her chair and picked up the phone to be vile to somebody else.

******

Lucy Makepeace kept her promise and Callery turned up for lunch the next day. She'd told him to come early, when the refectory was empty. As he approached the main doors Callery saw Adam Thicklow coming from the direction of the kitchens, holding a big mug. He halted momentarily when he noticed Callery, then smiled sheepishly and held the mug up.

'I just begged a tea bag from the kitchen girls,' he said. 'Ran out and I was desperate for a cuppa. Avoided Ms Moxey, luckily, she'd have slung me out.'

'Where do you eat, Mr Thicklow? Is it with the rest of the staff; I understand they eat at a separate table in the can – in the refectory?'

'Yeah, but I don't.' Thicklow looked down at his muddy boots. 'Non-teachers have to eat where they work, bring their own food.'

'That's a shame; the food here seems to be of a very high standard. In fact Ms Makepeace has invited me to join the lunch today.'

'Well you'll have a bloody good feed, I can tell you. Bon Appetit.'

Thicklow walked off. Callery went and gorged.

******

Lunch over, dishes dealt with and the kitchens swabbed down ready for the next day's assault, Sandra Moxey got the bus back to her small house on an newly-built estate outside Stuttenden. She went straight upstairs for a shower. Overalls off. The smell of large-scale catering was washed off her body, a quite nice lotion from Poundland smoothed on it instead, hair titivated, a good spray of last Christmas's present from her son - an online fake Chanel perfume and then… the smelly rotten kitchen overalls went back on. Sandra sighed. If only sex that paid had meant she could at least put on something clean, however cheap and tawdry. But this was the way her client – her particular client – wanted, always. And he was a very good payer, a very generous sum handed over immediately after the evening's shenanigans. Sandra didn't complain. She smeared on a smile with the new make-up, had a good swig of Baileys with vodka and Southern Comfort (all purloined from Stutters). Then she went downstairs and waited for the bell to ring at exactly half-past seven, which it always did. She opened the door and it revealed Orlando Fisham. It always did.

The usual events took place; there was a lot of swearing, slapping and insulting from Sandra Moxey and a great deal of ecstatic shouting, then whimpering, from Fisham. Twenty minutes later they were both lying back in Moxey's bed, smoking and drinking. She was now naked, Orlando was now wearing the kitchen overalls.

'You were a bit hard with me the other day, you know,' said Fisham. 'Bit near the knuckle with that You're going to lose your job stuff.'

Sandra Moxey looked surprised. 'You like me bein' rough with you! That's what you and me's all about, isn't it?'

'Yes. It is.'

'An' you love it,' said Moxey, leering at Fisham.

'I know. Oh, I think I'm always on edge with Perry and her rampaging ego. She's awful to work for.'

'Huh, try workin' for Makepeace!'

'And I don't like this detective hanging about either, asking questions and inferring things,' Fisham said.

''E don't know nothin',' said Sandra comfortably.

'Yes, but somebody killed Torbet, didn't they? And it's most likely one of us – followed her onto that boat and throttled her. Once he finds out there'll be a terrible scandal, the school could close; then what?'

Moxey stubbed out her cigarette and poured them both more of her personal mixture. 'He won't, there won't, it won't, so don't worry.'

'I'm not sure; he seems quite canny despite all that gangling daftness. I think he suspects me.'

A loud noise like a suddenly-unconstipated camel exploded in the room; it was Moxey laughing. 'You're not important enough to be a suspect, don't flatter yourself! Neither am I. 'E's after a bigger plot than the likes of us.'

Orlando Fisham despised Sandra Moxey, but he didn't underestimate her perspicacity. 'Who? You mean Perry?'

'Perry, one of the governors maybe, or a parent. Torbet was crafty, she knew lots, may 'ave made use of what she knew.'

Fisham lit them both more cigarettes. 'Well if Torbet had had anything on Perry I wouldn't be surprised if *she'd* bumped her off. No, that's no good, she's got an alibi.'

'She wouldn't stoop to doin' it herself! Pay somebody, she's got enough money.'

That worried Fisham even more. 'Who?'

Moxey pretended to inhale deeply; it fitted with her role as a débauchée. But she'd always been dead against smoking, a dope's way of paying governments she despised more money and what had killed her stupid old dad. She breathed in and then pursed her lips to expel nothing behind the smoke drifting unconsumed from her fag. Then she shrugged and leant over Fisham.

'Parents. Parents who don't need the money themselves, but theirs mean they've got the power, and influence. They can find people to do the rotten stuff, trust me.'

Orlando Fisham liked trusting Sandra. He also liked the next stage in their times together.

'Oh I don't want to think about it anymore. Is it time for – you know what?'

Moxey looked at her watch, a seriously expensive Rolex she only wore on these occasions, when she was with the generous giver. She often wondered how on earth he'd been able to afford it. 'It is. You know what to do.'

Orlando Fisham grinned and got out of bed. He dragged a coat over his cook's overalls and left to buy fish and chips from the van that called on the estate every Friday evening. Plenty of vinegar. And they'd need the leftover chips.

****

Callery had another go at some students. There must have been at least a few of them who'd noticed Torbet's little group of followers. He asked Perry for permission to talk to the last class Torbet had taken, the day before she'd left and boarded that ferry for France. He found himself in a very comfortable room along the corridor from Jeanne Torbet's in the Language Pod. It didn't have desks and a whiteboard for the teacher; it was furnished with plush armchairs, side tables, a stylish counter with what was no doubt a top of the range espresso machine and all that was needed for a superb cup of coffee, plus quality croissants and buns. Bloody hell, Callery thought as he sat on the edge of one of the curvy, velvet-covered chairs and faced a small group of self-possessed seventeen-year-olds. All boys, no girls. They lounged expectantly, as if he was a new pupil who wanted to be welcomed and liked.

'Hi,' he said. 'Thank you for agreeing to this chat. I'm interested in your impressions of Ms Torbet – what you thought of her as a teacher.'

There were several blank looks and a lot of shrugging.

'Didn't really know her,' one of the students said finally. 'She was just our teacher.'

'Tell me – you're all male. Was that usual, for classes to be divided this way? I thought that Stuttenden was proudly co-educational.'

Sniggers. 'It is when it suits the school to be,' said another of the group, a lanky boy draped over another of the luxurious armchairs.

'What do you mean?'

'Stutters is officially co-ed, but some of our parents – well, let's say they like the idea of their kids being at a mixed school but don't actually want us taught in the same room as… *women*.'

He widened his eyes in mock affront and there were joke gasps from the others.

'So you have French lessons, for instance, in single-sex classes?'

'We have *all* lessons apart from the girls – our stupid parents think it's more posh,' said a third boy moodily, leaning against the beverage counter. Knowing the ethos of this place Callery thought, it was probably called the Refreshment Capsule.

'And you mind that?'

There was another bit of shrugging. 'We manage to communicate in other ways – it's not a monastery.'

'I quite fancy nuns,' said the boy who'd spoken up first. They all laughed.

'Did Ms Torbet take any mixed classes, or were they all separated?'

'Yeah, she taught them as well. But she got paid extra for doing the split-up ones. All the teachers do. That's the deal, you see; the parents pay more – on top of the huge fees they pay to send us here anyway – for this separate stuff, that persuades the teachers to do it, even though the school's apparently a genuine mixed one.'

'Everyone keeps quiet about it – and everyone's happy,' said the youth in the armchair.

'Except us, the students! It's crazy.'

'But you just said that you get round the restriction,' said Callery, wishing he could get at those croissants.

'We do – but we shouldn't have to.'

'I've heard that with the girls' class Torbet had a sort – clique,' Callery dropped in. This provoked more cynical laughter.

'Yeah, you could say that.' This was from a boy who hadn't spoken before; a small, fair-haired figure huddled in another huge armchair, clutching a cup of coffee. He seemed younger than the others, but had a sort of old face.

'Would you say it?' asked Callery.

'Yes. Torbet was the kind of teacher who fostered that deliberately. You know, pick a few favourites and suck up to them, pretty much ignore the rest.'

'You seem to have a good idea of how the girls' class was.'

The old face smiled wryly. 'My sister's in it.'

Callery thought he'd like to talk to this sister. 'What's her name?'

'Emily.'

'Thank you—?'

'Me? I'm Thomas.'

Callery stood up. 'Thankyou everybody. You've all been very helpful.'

He left the group still lounging and went in search of lunch.

****

Callery left the school grounds and made for the village centre. It wasn't far of course; Stuttenden school loomed like a cathedral; it was vital to the village, but it couldn't survive without the village. It was like a huge worm, feeding from the body it needed, giving and taking – rending and sucking. It was awful. Callery went into the shop, grabbed a wire basket and went round the tightly-packed aisles trying to find what he only needed; sandwiches, loads of 'em. Maybe some Scotch eggs. A bottle of water – crisps, ordinary ones, if this poncey place had them as well as the over-priced Shredz. He was happy to run into Lisa Choke again, though.

'Well here you are, Mr Detective. Local talk is that you haven't got any forwarder with your work here?' Lisa smiled as Callery reached the cash desk and started taking his items from the basket. 'Eating alone again?'

Callery felt happy to see her, relaxed that she was a normal person with no ulterior motive like everybody at Stuttenden but also a bit threatened. Lisa Choke *was* normal, she chatted, she joked – and she flirted.

'Erm, yes. Got any sausage rolls?'

'Course we have.' Lisa smiled even more and looked at the heated unit, glowing with pasties – beef or cheese and onion – and sausage rolls. She knew Callery had seen it the first time he'd been into the shop; he knew she knew it. Callery felt a complete fool; he also felt desperate for food.

'Oh, right – yeah. Some of them, please.'

Lisa Choke was perfectly professional. She took up the metal prongs needed, plucked three – no, Callery said make it four – sausage rolls from the heater and bagged them up for him. He reminded himself that she'd been very nice and open the first time he'd been in the shop.

'Thank you. That's very kind of you – Lisa, isn't it? You're quite right, we're – it's not going as smoothly as we'd hoped.'

Callery was glad Ms. Choke didn't probe about his background; he hated talking about himself, asking questions was what he was used to, not answering them. But she was obviously keen to know what he thought of the village as opposed to the school.

'How you finding it, Mr. Policeman? Comfy enough at the pub?'

'Yeah, it's good,' he replied. 'Bed's a bit short, but then they always are for me. Grub's decent and enough of it, nice staff – yeah, it's alright there.'

'Good,' said Lisa, putting more pasties under the heat lamp. She looked meaningfully at Callery. 'There was a murder *there*, y'know.'

'Really? When?' Callery's brain perked up at this.

'Oh ever so long ago, in 1970 I think, this was before the school opened. My auntie remembers it – she had a Saturday job shelf-stackin' in here.'

'What happened?'

'The landlord did his brother in – reckoned the brother was playin' around with the landlord's wife. Bludgeoned 'im to death with an axe from the woodshed outside – ooh it was terrible, my auntie said.'

'Did this landlord have any family – kids, I mean, who stayed here so he'd have descendants in the village today?' Callery was thinking; could one killer hanging off the family tree mean another fifty years later?

Lisa Choke shrugged. 'Dunno. My auntie said the wife left the village after he got jailed for the murder, I'm not sure about kids.'

A descendant could always come back, pretend to have no connection with the village. Lisa was still chatting on.

'The brewery wanted to change the name, thought the Haunted Chimney would have people thinkin' the brother's ghost would be roamin' the place, but the village campaigned to keep it. You got all you want?'

Callery paid, gasped inwardly at the cost of a few bits for lunch, said goodbye and went to sit in the cemetery of the church to eat.

After scoffing his lunch amongst the gravestones Callery decided to have a go at more pupils. There was an art class starting at two o'clock, so he loped along to the Visual Arts Cell at ten past. Cell it wasn't; seven teenagers clad in immaculate white coats were spread out in a huge, airy space with a ceiling that was all skylight; the brightness was clear and glorious.

Orlando Fisham had been informed of Callery's visit, but he still looked petrified as Callery approached him standing by one girl's easel. Then the fear turned into petulance.

'For god's sake – what now?' Fisham growled, clutching a paintbrush as if he wanted to shove it down Callery's throat.

'Don't worry, Mr Fisham,' said Callery lightly. 'I'm not here for you; I'd just like to have another chat with some of your students – if that's all right with you?'

Fisham's grip on the brush of death relaxed a bit. 'Okay,' he said cautiously, then turned and called to the whole class. 'Take a break, kids, this – the Detective Inspector would like to talk to you again about the— the terrible recent event in our school.' Fisham slipped out of the room and the seven pupils looked alert, as if being talked to by a policeman was going to be a sight more interesting than trying to emulate Damien Hirst.

'Okay,' Callery began in a bright, strong voice. 'If you'd like to gather round, get a bit closer – this is just an informal chat, I'm not here to interrogate any of you—'

The students gathered, but not near Callery; they all made for an enormous, scruffy grey sofa by one of the windows and collapsed into that. It was as if they'd fallen against the flaccid body of an old, dead elephant. Callery had to go over to them. There were five girls and two boys; the lads immediately lit up and after a couple of passed-around puffs Callery could definitely smell weed. Right, this was how they wanted to play it, arrogant little bastards. Well they'd be disappointed, he wasn't bothered with dodgy fags so there'd be no affronted speech about how he could arrest them all, this was out of order. He knew that was what they wanted, so that well-connected parents and high-powered lawyers could be immediately involved and he would be rebuffed and humiliated. They could smoke cannabis as much as they liked.

'Do you enjoy your art classes?' Callery started in a roundabout way.

There was the same silence as in the Language Pod first off, then one of the boys who'd started the smoking took another gasping lungful, passed the joint to the girl squashed next to him and spoke.

'Not much. But if it means we don't have to do more chemistry that's fine by us.' The girls giggled like a backing group.

'None of you is particularly interested in a career in the fine arts, then?'

One of the backing group piped up. 'I'd like to sell art, in an auction house. My uncle is head of the Early Italian Renaissance department at Christie's.'

Well that's your life sorted, Callery thought.

'I *am* an artist,' another girl said challengingly. 'As soon as I leave school and get away from this meretricious hole and collaborate with Owusu in Ghana I'm off. He lives in a shanty town and teaches children to read.'

'Really?' Callery was impressed; this sounded independent and adventurous, even altruistic.

'Yeah,' joined in the second boy with a sarcastic smile that still made him look gorgeous. 'Abeiku Owusu was in our class until last term. His father's the High Commissioner to London, Ab turns up at the shanty town once a week to update his Facebook page and the rest of the time flits between a penthouse in Accra and his mum's place in Geneva. His last Instagram post showed us him and his ma slurping homemade pasta with Sophia Loren. Stop pretending to be humble, Emily.'

Aah, this was Emily, the sister of the old-faced boy, Callery surmised. There were loads of Emilys in the school, but he bet this one was who he'd like to talk further to. Come to think of it, she did have the same look of elderly wisdom hanging about her smooth blonde features.

'Have you got a brother named Thomas?'

The old look deepened. 'Yes. Why?'

'I was talking to him and his classmates about Jeanne Torbet this morning, that's all. They were very helpful.'

'We can be,' rejoined Emily, 'What exactly do you want to know? If you've spoken to Tom's class what more could we tell you?'

'Well for a start, how many of you also had French lessons with Ms Torbet?'

Five hands went up, languorously. All the girls, including Emily.

'Did you like her as a teacher?'

'Some of us did.' This was from another of the backing group cushioned in the elephant.

'Did you? ...Sorry, your name is?'

'Jessica. Jessica Chant-Lewis. Yeah, I did. She was great. If you wanted to really learn French – not just the language, if she saw you were keen she'd explain the culture, the politics, the whole ethos of the country, she bothered to give us extra lessons after the school day, me and the others, it – it was brilliant. It made us want to live in France, *be* French. I miss it. I hate this country.'

There was more sniggering, from the first boy. 'Oh come off it Jess, you only want to get out because you can see that Tom's going to be running Britain in twenty years' time and still be bossing you about as well as the rest of us.' The joint came back to him and he took another strong inward hissful.

'I enjoyed learning French, but I hated her.' This was from yet another of the girls, a dark-haired beauty with sultry eyes who'd probably be well-married, plump and boring by thirty. Or head of the EU. Or both. Callery's head was starting to spin with the concept of just how much these young people would be able to achieve. It was like swimming with baby sharks.

'Ah – why?' Callery tried to resist the eyes.

'Well, Bryant's right, Jess is a disaffected twig off her family's branch. She doesn't want to be part of the hierarchy she's been born into, but I do. And Ms Torbet was great at making us all aware of that, the possibilities.'

Right, the EU. 'Yes?' said Callery encouragingly.

'Yes. She was a great teacher. But she was fickle. She liked you – really liked you – and then she didn't. You know; she was a stirrer, she liked her pupils to compete and fall out, she liked a disturbing atmosphere. I'm – sorry, I'm glad she's dead. My turn, Bry.'

Sultry eyes squinted as the joint was handed over and a huge drag taken from it. Callery felt more confused than ever; Torbet was unliked by the staff but had an adoring little family to gather round her. Except that some in the family weren't adoring, they loathed the head of it. Where the hell was the killer of Jeanne Torbet? Was it at Stuttenden? Was it in France where Torbet was headed, that fateful day on the ferry? Was it somewhere else, nothing to do with her job or private life? What – or who - was she? Callery was stumped, and felt that he was supposed to be stumped. By the mystery that Torbet had left behind her.

Chapter Six

Two days later Callery was invited to the school's summer party –
but on the proviso that he masqueraded as a teacher. Anishka Perry
tried to make him impersonate Hanna Fischer's assistant in German
Studies with perfect English, but Callery balked at that and agreed to
lurk as some sort of assistant in the Science Department. So he lurked,
glass of excellent wine in hand and his ears straining for any scrap of
conversation that touched on Jeanne Torbet and her killing. Perry had
deputed Lou Shelbourne to appear with Callery at the beginning and
usher him into the Stuttenden world of wealth and ease.

'How do you like pretending to be a teacher, Mr Detective?' asked
Lou, hiding her voice and a grin behind a large glass of the same wine
he'd got.

'I don't, not much. But it's a good opportunity to listen, maybe hear
more about Torbet from people outside the school.'

'Good plan. I suppose we should just chat as employees, both
working for our illustrious head in our different, challenging ways?'

Callery felt free to talk off the record, even though anything he was
told would, of course, be straight back on it. 'You must come across
some of these parents, don't they always have gripes about their
offspring not being treated fairly?'

'Genius under-appreciated, inabilities treated insensitively, you
mean? No, we don't get much of that, it's usually moaning about the
food, or too much term time stopping their darlings being taken out of
school for lengthy exotic holidays.'

'The food? What's wrong with that? I've never eaten such good
grub.'

'I agree. But you see, the more money and privilege people have, the more they want. These parents, they can't bear conceding anything. They pay vast amounts of money for a "good" education for their kids, but they only want it the way it suits. They can't accept not calling the shots. Yes, the food is exceptional. But they're paying for the ability to criticise it.'

Callery looked at Lou Shelbourne. For once her smiling countenance looked ever so slightly cynical.

'*Is* it a good education?'

Lou shrugged. 'It can be; some of the teachers are great, as far as I can gather. Fischer, Bianchi and Abreu are. Hayes is decent – Torbet was good too, I think, going by A-level results. My boss was always happy with that, whatever Torbet was like as a person, despite her coldness.'

'Do you like working at this school, Ms Shelbourne?'

'I thought we were supposed to be just chatting in a superficial way, *Mr* Callery?'

'Quite right.' Callery realised he'd been probing too much, rather than just looking round with a bit of meaningless talk going on for appearances' sake. He changed tack.

'Are you from this area?'

Lou shook her head as she swallowed a good glug of wine. 'North London, me. Highgate. After Uni I travelled a bit, then came home and couldn't decide what to do next. Started PA-ing, then my uncle got me in here.'

'Your uncle?'

'He's one of the governors.'

'Aha.' Callery rolled up this possibly interesting little piece of knowledge and tucked it away. 'And life in north London, family?'

'Ma and Pops? Ma has this really successful online garden supply company – it's crazy, she literally started it with a tray of seedlings on the kitchen windowsill!'

'And your father?'

'Dad? Oh we don't see anything of him, he just provided the seed.' Lou paused. 'Huh, maybe that's why Ma went into gardening – y'know, control seeds herself from then on. No, Pops is Poppy, my other ma.'

Callery made himself be modern and fine, although he felt old and left behind. 'Right, okay. But the— the conception in a toil—'

'Oh that, yes that was the required biological twosome. Dad was on call when Ma needed to procreate and she liked to make an occasion of it. Then he went back to being Richard's butler on Necker.'

A waiter-borne tray passed. Callery grabbed two more glasses; he and Lou plonked their empty ones onto it in exchange.

'So, brothers or sisters…?'

'Only Roof.'

Callery waited for what was coming, but tried. 'Short for Rufus?'

'No, just Roof. Where he was con—'

A parent lurched up, obviously drunk already. 'Ms Shelbourne, how nice to see you! Making sure our marvellous Ms Perry is free to headline these prestigious events? Before she moves on to greater office?'

It was said lightly, but with malice underneath. Lou Shelbourne smiled sweetly, then said she had to check on catering arrangements and moved away. Callery carried on listening to the awful woman for a few minutes, then escaped by taking her drained glass and promising to return with it replenished. As if. He mingled, which is what he should have done from the start.

Few of the parents, except the ones whose kids were taking French, seemed to have known much about Torbet when alive. But dead she was absolutely fascinating; they couldn't stop asking - in what they thought were hushed, diplomatic tones but were actually rasping and insistent – What Really Happened. Perry had instructed her staff to give reserved answers and turn the questions back on the askers; your child is so bright and perceptive, so good at languages, what have they conveyed to *you?*

Not much, it appeared. One or two parents said they reckoned it was to do with drugs, Torbet had probably been a smuggler and got herself into trouble with the "gang", one of whom had bumped her off. A particularly dense pupil with a particularly wealthy mum and dad (they'd started an online pet funeral business and recently sold it to a Chinese conglomerate for unimaginable millions) had told them that Torbet had "prob'ly died of starvation, innit?"

The parents whose kids had been pupils of Torbet, conversely, possibly knew more but were very reticent.

'Camomile adored her,' said one thin, brittle-faced woman who looked grossly disappointed with life (Callery later found out that she was the founder of a spectacularly successful sex gadget company, had a personal fortune of sixty million pounds, four gorgeous children and an independently successful husband who adored her. And she made smashing cakes, at home).

'Yes,' said Callery leadingly. 'Ms Torbet seemed to have a— a group of favoured pupils who she was close to, who— they were very integrated into their lessons.'

Brittleness broke and a huge smile covered the taut face. 'Oh yes! To whom Ms Torbet was close yes, that's exactly how it was, our darling Cammy was genetically prohibited to absorb any language skills and then, in Jeanne's class she just— she burst into being able to speak and learn and be interested in life! I'm telling you, that woman was such a good teacher – and revered for it.'

'Right,' said Callery cautiously. 'Torbet seemed to have quite a small class in that respect – six girls?'

The brittleness came back. 'That's what we pay for, what Stuttenden supplies; the best possible education in a micro-endemic development enhancement experience. The prospectus says so.'

'Yeah, right…'Callery tailed off, baffled.

'Sorry, and you teach what exactly?'

'Er, science – physics, with an internet sort of leaning… Hey, the Head's going to make a speech—'

Callery was saved by Anishka Perry's desire to speak in public and further her path to government. The thin ludicrously wealthy woman who'd very nearly exposed Callery suddenly had a beatific smile on her face, gazing like all the other parents at Perry orating whilst glasses were filled yet again with champagne. Callery thanked Perry for the fact that her ambition had let him off the hook and escaped to the back of the crowd, grabbing another glass of wine on the way.

The back was where he found himself standing by a beautiful black woman. Tall, slim and curvy and elegant and voluptuous and approachable and forbidding and everything, all at the same time. She was smiling too, but somehow not like the parents; her grin was knowing, normal, outside of this school and its controlling atmosphere. She made him smile in return.

'Hi,' he said.

'Hi. Enjoying yourself?' she said back.

'Yeah. Yes. I— I'm a new teacher here, starting next term, here to get acquainted and all that – and you are?'

'Carmen Moseki. I never met Jeanne Torbet, I know nothing about her, I was chairing a seminar in Liverpool the day she was killed and my alibi has already been cleared by your police force – Inspector Callery? Since when did policemen teach in disgustingly wealthy private schools?

'Ah, you know who I am.'

'I do,' said the woman with that great, uncomplicated smile still on her attractive face. 'How is your enquiry going – am I allowed to ask that?'

'I suppose so. It's— we're making progress.' Callery swallowed the fib with a big glug of Sancerre.

'Oh dear.' The smile bubbled over into a laugh that Callery should have felt offended by, but wasn't; he laughed too.

'No honestly,' he bluffed. 'It's difficult, but I am getting there. I will get there. What do you teach?'

'Right, don't ask any more questions about the murder. History.'

'Ah! Then can I ask you something that's nothing to do with the murder either? Why – *why* do historians on TV or the radio always talk about the past in the present tense?'

'How do you mean?'

'Just that; they always talk about, say, Charles the Second in the sixteenth century—'

'Seventeenth.'

'Sorry, the seventeenth – why do they *always* say things like Charles the Second *goes* to France to meet Louis and the two of them *have* a walk in the gardens at Versailles and Charles feels very suspicious about Louis' motives – stuff like that happened nearly three hundred years ago—'

'Four hundred.'

'Right, sorry – why do they do it? It's not going on now, is it? It happened all that time ago, it's *in the past.*'

'Was.'

'Eh?'

'It was in the past. You used the present tense. About the past.'

Callery could see that the piss was being taken – charmingly – out of him. He changed the subject back to the murder.

'How much contact did you have with Jeanne Torbet?'

'Oh, so now we *can* talk about the case. I told you; none. We didn't teach the same subject so we didn't have the same students, we lived in different parts of the village and had nothing in common socially.'

'Your paths really never crossed?'

Carmen Moseki shook her head and held up her glass. 'We were at the same occasions like this, standing around drinking this stuff while our esteemed head practised being Home Secretary, but I honestly never spoke one word to her. Now, can I ask you something?'

'Of course.' Callery was really enjoying himself.

'Why, in television dramas, does every single character being interviewed use the detective's name all the time? It drives me mad!'

Callery imagined Carmen Moseki, mad and lively. He had to switch that off and listen. 'What do you mean?'

'Well, whenever anybody's being going to be asked about the murder, when the police first meet them they say things like How can I help you, Chief Inspector; then they say would you like a cup of tea Chief Inspector, and when it gets a bit dodgy they say I haven't the foggiest idea Chief Inspector and when the detective leaves they say goodbye I'm sorry I couldn't help you further, Chief Inspector. Why do they do that? I mean, we don't use titles all the time like that – I don't say good morning, Head of School to Perry whenever I meet her, can I speak with you later Head of School, would you like me to take that extra class Head of School – it's ridiculous!'

Callery tried to stop himself being entranced by Ms Moseki's flashing eyes and gorgeous, expressive mouth. 'I'm only a Detective Inspector.'

'Oh. Sorry. But it's the same thing – you don't get called Detective Inspector all the time, do you?'

'I get called a lot worse. But yeah, yeah they do, don't they. I don't know, all those cop shows are rubbish.'

'I'm sorry,' said Ms Moseki again. 'I'm being fatuous; you have a real live murder to solve. Sorry, live murder, that's rubbish too.'

She looked apologetically at Callery for an instant, then burst out laughing. He laughed too.

'Hey, this is empty—'

Callery took Ms Moseki's glass and went in search of a waiter.

But when he came back with two refilled glasses Moseki was deep in conversation with what was probably a parent. Callery handed her her glass and then hovered, miserable again and listening, trying to look as though he wasn't. And then Anishka Perry approached and granted him a few minutes of her gilded presence and time.

'Do you know the school motto?' She asked with a smile that was obviously supposed to be appealing, even flirty, but compared to Carmen Moseki's was like a snake eyeing up a baby mongoose.

'No,' said Callery. 'I never did Latin.'

Perry snorted. 'It's not Latin you need to understand our slogan, it's economics. "Scientia Et Patria".'

'Which is?' Callery asked with a sigh. She'd just said he didn't need Latin but here she was, showing hers off to him.

'"Knowledge And Country". Sounds patriotic, doesn't it? It's not. What it means for the parents who send their offspring here is gain the knowledge you need in order to make as much as you can from this country. Learn only what's necessary to shaft everyone else in the UK.'

'That's very cynical.'

'No it's not, it's honest. I know that's what the kids who come here are supposed to leave with; a desire to make money easily – and not much else. I *should* know; I've got that work ethic myself.'

'Then Ms Torbet's… well, grasping attitude – would have meant she fitted in very neatly here?'

'She suited the school perfectly in that respect. But as I told you – and I'm sure, as many of my staff have told you – she didn't try to fit in with anything else.'

'Did you know anything about her private life?'

'No. We hold a highly enjoyable Christmas evening for the teachers, just after the school has closed for the holidays and all the students have left; it's a chance for everyone to relax and really mingle. Partners are welcome, to add to the variety and emphasise the complete informality of the occasion.'

Callery felt as though he was being sold the school in order that he'd send his kids to it. 'That must be nice.'

'Torbet never produced anyone. She would stay for my speech and the starter, then leave. I think that tells you all. And now I must leave you and mix. Feel free to stay and be un-Torbetlike.'

Anishka Perry laughed lightly at her own joke, then moved off. Callery took another glass of wine from a passing tray and lurked in the vicinity of more parents.

He managed to hear the conversation of two men, casually but expensively dressed, drinking beer not champagne from a stylish beer tent that Perry had agreed to be set up at the edge of the lawn. Callery yearned for a glass but had been instructed by Perry that, as a supposed junior member of staff he had to stick to wine. He guessed later that Perry had insisted on this to keep some of the jollier, more loquacious fathers from chatting openly to him.

'Well I reckon it's time to get out,' one of the men was slurrily saying to the other, jabbing a finger in the air to make his point.

'Yeah?' said the second man, just as fuzzily.

'Yep. The usual stuff, I can put up with that, but a bloody murder – nah, not good, time to pull away.'

'You're probably right.'

'I am! Am, mate. Time to go.'

''nother pint?'

'Yeah, c'mon.' The two men lurched off. Callery saw Orlando Fisham nearby and nabbed him.

'Tell me, Mr Fisham, do you know who those people are? Parents?'

Fisham squinted, then shuddered. 'The taller one owns a highly successful brewery; he's responsible for that garish tent affair dispensing ale. The other one I'm not sure about but I've seen him at parents' evenings with a strikingly dull woman I would make a determined effort to avoid, however rich and well-connected.'

'They have kids at Stutters?' asked Callery.

'I'm afraid to say yes, they do. I hate my job.' Fisham was sad and drunk so of no use to Callery today. He gave up and went to the pub for food.

He pushed the door open and found he'd have to squeeze himself in. The place was packed; the bar was clustered with casually well-dressed men and women eager for new drinks or fresh ones, waving bank cards to try and get the staff's attention. Every stylishly-upholstered armchair around the crackling log fire had somebody in it, clutching a long glass of something or a pint. Callery got to the end of the bar and loomed over it; as soon as one of the five teenagers serving got near he asked for a Guinness and the menu. He wanted to escape to the restaurant part and order, but reckoned he'd better stay stuck in the bar and try to get talking; everybody in this pub would either be a parent with a child at Stutters or work there.

He took his drink over to the fireplace and hung around it, trying to find a vaguely familiar face without looking as though he was looking. He found one: Everard Hayes, chatting away in a corner to – of all people! – Sandra Moxey. She had a tray full of empty glasses in her hands and was, unbelievably, smiling. It was a pleasant, genuine smile, not a contemptuous grin at somebody else's misfortune. Callery took a deep breath and approached the two of them.

'Inspector!' Hayes seemed genuinely glad to see him. Sandra Moxey's bright expression curdled into her usual sneer.

'Mr Hayes… Ms Moxey.' Callery nodded twice, then took a gulp of Guinness. Hayes finished his drink and put the glass on Moxey's tray.

''nother one, Mr Hayes? I'm taking these back anyway.'

'Thank you, Sandra. The usual very large G and T, put it on my tab. Get one yourself. Inspector?'

Before Callery could answer no, he was fine at the moment, Sandra Moxey moved away. If he had wanted another pint he'd have had to get it himself, obviously.

'This place is very busy,' said Callery. 'Is it always like this?'

'When we have a parents' evening yes,' said Hayes. 'But generally speaking it's pretty popular from every Friday to Sunday. The village pub – the village – couldn't do without Stutters.'

'Could Stutters do without the village pub?'

Hayes snorted. 'Well I certainly couldn't! And I'm not the only teacher on the payroll who needs to come here at the end of the day.'

'Oh yeah? Who else is a regular?'

'Most of the English staff. The science lot, although they tend to pop in for a couple of pints at lunchtime, not evenings. Perry doesn't, except at Christmas when she treats us all.'

'Did Torbet come in much?'

Hayes shook his head. 'No. No, she didn't. Torbet liked to go home and have wine with dinner, I think – sorry, I'm being stereotypical. Brits in the pub, Continentals chez nous.'

'Chez who?'

'Forget it, never was any good at languages except my own. Ah, here comes Sandra—'

Moxey approached bearing a very generous glassful with ice clinking against two wedges of lemon.

'Ooh and look, lemons, you've included dinner as well!' Hayes took the glass and a big mouthful.

'Stop it,' said Sandra Moxey. 'Lemon's not food, you never eat enough. You should go into the restaurant and eat some pasta or something to mop that up.' She sounded quite concerned.

'I will, I will,' said Hayes.

'Actually I was thinking of going through to order,' said Callery. 'Would you like to join me?'

And to his surprise Everard Hayes said yes.

'You're good friends with Sandra Moxey?' Callery asked after they'd ordered; a starter portion of ravioli for Hayes and a large lasagne with double garlic bread for Callery.

Hayes thought for a moment. 'I don't know if I'd say we were *friends*,' he replied, waving his empty glass at a passing waitress for replenishment. 'We share a similarly healthy cynicism towards our employers. To the world in general, perhaps.'

'She's certainly been cynical when talking to me,' Callery said gloomily. 'Bloody rude, in fact.'

Hayes laughed. 'Don't take it personally, Sandra's like that with everybody.'

'She seems to be quite caring about you, fretting about you eating enough.'

Hayes shrugged. 'She works in catering; food is what she provides. But you're right in a way, I suppose. She does bother about me more than anyone else at the school.'

'And why do think that is?' Hayes' drink and the garlic bread arrived; Hayes took a big gulp from his glass, Callery tore a big chunk off and shoved it into his mouth.

'I think that maybe it's because we all hate Perry but suck up to her in public, but I'm the only one who'll admit in private what a hypocrite I am. The others tie themselves in knots justifying their sycophancy.'

'And Ms Moxey approves of that?'

'Sandra approves of anything that doesn't smack of pusillanimity. She likes confrontation.' Hayes drank deeply again.

'Really? Would you say that she'd be prepared to take revenge for something that she took personally?'

'Oh definitely. You should hear about some of the fights that have gone on in the kitchens.'

'Actual fights?'

Hayes smiled lasciviously and widened his eyes. 'Down to torn overalls and exposed nipples.'

'Blimey.'

'Indeed. No wonder she got fired from her last job.'

'Yeah? What was that?'

Hayes lowered his voice, even though the noise in the pub was reaching eleven in volume. 'She was a cleaner on the ferries. From Dover to Calais. Bit of a coincidence, given Torbet's place of demise.'

Callery's brain whirled. He didn't even finish the last piece of garlic bread on his plate. Everard Hayes finished his G and T.

'I think I'll have the same again,' he said, waving his glass at a passing waiter.

'I would too,' said Callery. 'But I've suddenly got work to do.'

Chapter Seven

This was a stunner. Sandra Moxey, belligerent, bitter – and violent – was now revealed as having worked on ferries that plied the exact same route that Jeanne Torbet had taken… and met her killer. Moxey would have made – well, if not friends, contacts on those crossings. Contacts who might need the money and would be paid to bump somebody off. Or were threatened themselves with dire consequences unless they did what Moxey said. She'd kept quiet about this job, deliberately. Callery would have to get hold of Moxey the very next morning and challenge her – not a prospect he relished.

He left The Haunted Chimney early the next day and got to the school's kitchens just as the doors were opened to admit the staff. Women, old and young, trickled in, chatting and laughing. The laughter was probably because it was a Friday. Callery followed them and made for Sandra Moxey's office. She was already there, frowning at the screen of her computer. The frown deepened when she looked up and saw Callery.

'What? I'm busy.'

'I want a serious word with you, Ms Moxey,' Callery said with what he hoped sounded like menace. He stood over Moxey and for once was glad he was so ridiculously tall.

'What about?' Sandra had to put her head right back to look up at Callery's looming figure.

'About the fact that you used to work for the same ferry company whose boat Jeanne Torbet was on when she was murdered.'

'So? I don't work there no more, do I? I was 'ere when she was done in, this is my job now.'

'That doesn't matter. You have a direct connection with the crime scene; you could still have contacts on that boat, someone who could have killed Torbet at your behest.'

'At my what?' Moxey was as belligerent as ever, but she appeared a bit rattled now.

'Why didn't you tell me this when I first interviewed you? Not doing so incriminates you and could make you a prime suspect, Ms Moxey.'

'Look, I left the ferries three years ago, I don't know no-one there now. You keep askin' me stuff – you're persecutin' me.'

Callery smiled – sinisterly, he hoped. 'I could be *charging* you very soon, Ms Moxey,' he said quietly. 'We'll discuss this further – when I've checked with the ferry company about your time there.'

Sandra Moxey looked sullen, like a rebuked student. Callery walked out. As he left he heard a ping on Moxey's computer – presumably an email – and her responding growl. He got straight on the phone and asked his so-called team to speak to someone at the company to verify Moxey's date of departure and exactly why she was sacked – what the supposed fight had been about. To his surprise, Callery's request was dealt with swiftly; Moxey *had* been involved in a tussle with another cleaner about overtime and had had her employment terminated when she'd said. She'd been as abrasive there as she was now at Stuttenden school and hadn't made any friends. In fact one member of staff, when questioned, made a point of saying how unpleasant Sandra Moxey had been to work with and that, since she'd gone, the crew members who remained had all agreed that they'd never wanted to have anything to do with her again. And it hadn't been a really nasty fight; Moxey had lost her job because she'd also been found to have stolen industrial-sized cleaning products, probably for resale. There'd been no tearing of overalls, no exposed nipples. Hayes had just been fantasising.

****

Joy of joys, Sergeant Peattie rang one morning and said he was in the area, could get to Canterbury; was Callery free for a pint? Callery definitely was. He went to the ancient city with enough time to visit the cathedral before meeting Peattie at the entrance, as arranged. After ambling down the long high street he tried to find the church, but it wasn't so easy for a non-local. Oh he could *see* it, he just couldn't get there; it loomed over everything, but where the bloody actual entrance was stayed away, a luring mystery. In the end Callery asked a shop owner chatting in his doorway to a woman with a dog; the man and the woman laughed, probably because they found it funny that outsiders didn't know exactly where the most famous monument in Canterbury was. The man pointed up the road to a square and said it's *there,* as if Callery was an idiot. As Callery walked off he was sure the dog was laughing too. The square had presumably been the original heart of Canterbury, earliest habitats huddled up against the gates that led into the church grounds. It was as if the cathedral itself was a giant tree, soaring above the settlement, the houses clustered near like mushrooms at the tree's foot. Callery bought a ticket and entered. Immediately inside the grounds was like a separate, private town with houses – offices now, probably – edging wide lawns that surrounded the magnificent edifice he'd just paid ten quid to see. Tourists milled about pointing phones at anything. Callery went in; a helpful guide came up and offered to give him an introduction to the cathedral. She told him that some of the stone used to build the church had been brought from Normandy by William The Conqueror once he'd taken over Kent. More France, Callery thought, I can't get away from it – and I can't get to it either.

It was impressive though, he thought, after the guide had finished her speech and he was strolling about, his head permanently crooked up to gaze at the incredible vaulting. Callery didn't believe in God – he didn't believe in anything except extra-large portions – but there was a sort of awe-inspiring atmosphere about this place that he enjoyed being affected by. It was so different from his usual state of mind; cynicism, suspicion and contempt. He let himself be awed for another half an hour or so then emerged. Peattie was waiting.

'How come you're in this neck of the woods?' asked Callery, after they grinned broadly at each other, shook hands and started for the nearest pub. As soon as they found a decently archaic one, half-timbered outside and shabbily cosy inside, they entered, ordered pints and fish and chips and settled into chairs near the woodburner.

'Oh family stuff,' Peattie had replied on the way and then changed the subject to general police gossip. Like Callery – like blokes – he wanted to be in a pub with a pint, then would be the time to chat. Now they were safely ensconced he elaborated. 'Wife's nephew's wedding; he lives in Faversham. When I realised that's not far from where you are I thought well, it'd be nice to meet up with my old boss for a bit of a natter and a pint or two. How's it goin', sir?'

Callery wanted to tell Peattie he shouldn't call him sir anymore, now that he was no longer his sergeant. Peattie had stayed on when Callery had been transferred and was studying for his Inspector's exams. But Callery didn't; he knew that Peattie would say sir without thinking and telling him not to would seem as if Callery was assuming the authority he no longer had. Peattie wasn't his assistant now, he was his mate. And a mate was who you confided in.

'I tell you, it's driving me mad. This school, it's— everybody in it is— oh I dunno, they're all falsifying somehow, they're not who they want me to think they are.'

'Hmm,' said Peattie after a good glug of beer. 'You mean they all seem like suspects?'

'No, not exactly.' Callery matched Peattie gulp for gulp and shoved in a few fistfuls of crisps to keep him going until the fish and chips arrived. 'Well they are, of course, you're right, until I know who's done it they all have, in a way, any one of 'em – but I meant they're *all* dishonest, automatically. They don't trust me – that's okay, we're never the most popular of people are we, turning up and asking hard questions, accusing everybody – but they don't even seem to trust each other! They're all— all on edge, all the time. I don't want to be there.'

'You'll solve it, sir, I'm sure. Wife's family know of it of course, said it's a lovely village, out of their league as far as property's concerned – and the school itself what you'd dream of for your kids.'

'You wouldn't Peattie, I'm telling you. These children come from everything, they get given everything at Stutters, but even they aren't happy. There's something… something *diseased* about the place.'

'Blimey. Makes Habbabenleigh sound pleasant.'

Callery growled. 'Don't remind me.'

'I wonder how they all are,' said Peattie ponderingly. 'What they're all doing now.'

'Well Mrs Tapp's doing the rest of her sentence, as far as I know,' said Callery.

He drained his glass and was about to take it with Peattie's to the bar when lunch turned up, brought by a sweet teenager who looked too young and small to manage the vast plates she was bearing. She smiled in relief when Callery and Peattie took them from her and was only too glad to get their second pints for them, scuttling off like a happy mouse.

'Have you got anyone in mind for this murder, sir?'

'That's the trouble – like I said, all of 'em in a way. Well, not the ones who've got concrete alibis of course, but the ones that haven't could all be in the frame. Oh let's not discuss it now, Peattie, let's forget work.'

Nothing of anything was said for the next ten minutes. Then the two men sighed and sat back from cleared plates with their drinks.

'How's the studying going?' Callery asked.

Peattie nodded. 'Not bad, not too bad. Course it helps with the technology we've got now, there's none of that trawlin' through evidence packed into loads of boxes or goin' to the library or lectures like it used to be. It's all online now – I can work when I want, where I want; home mostly, which is great.'

Callery snorted. 'Technology, that's another thing I don't trust.'

Peattie couldn't help it. 'Do you text, sir?'

'Only when I have to.'

'Facebook?'

'Nope.'

'Twitter?'

'Nope.'

Peattie started enjoying this. 'Instagram?'

'What?'

'Pinterest?'

'Eh?'

'Would you say you're ever influenced by Influencers? Heard of TikTok?'

'I've got a watch… Peattie, what the hell are you talking about?'

Peattie was smiling broadly by now. 'But sir, you email, don't you? I mean you have to, submit reports and that.' Mind you, he suddenly thought, I used to do most of those, didn't I? Peattie started to wonder if Callery could actually read or write.

'Peattie, go and get two more pints,' Callery grumbled.

'Yes sir.'

Peattie did and came back with two bowls of apple pie and custard as well, so Callery forgot to grumble and shovelled his huge share down.

'That's better,' he said after thirty seconds of eating. 'I'd still felt peckish somehow after the fish and chips – I reckon that girl gave us child's portions.'

Peattie was only half way through his. Between mouthfuls he asked Callery who he had on his list of suspects and Callery obliged with swift descriptions of Perry, Fisham, Hayes, Makepeace, Thicklow and Moxey and their possible motives. The descriptions were vivid, but the supposed motives were wobbly.

'And if you *had* to pick one, who would you go for, sir?'

Callery groaned. 'Oh god… I think I'd go for Sandra Moxey.'

'The cook?'

'Yeah… she's as false as the others but without the paranoia. And she lied – well, she withheld a vital piece of information.' Callery described Hayes' revelation and the subsequent conversation with Moxey about working on the ferries. The thought of it still made him shudder.

'And what would be her why, sir?'

Callery groaned again. 'I haven't a clue, Peattie me old mate. She—she hated Torbet, she had a mate who still worked on the ferries and she paid them to throttle her. Or Torbet had something on Moxey – blackmail – and Moxey had to have Torbet silenced.'

'I have to say sir,' said Peattie reluctantly, 'That it sounds a bit far-fetched.'

'Far-fetched? It's ridiculous! Come on, I'll get us more pints.'

The two men drank, then left the pub and wandered around Canterbury a bit in the late afternoon sunshine until Peattie had to get his train home. Callery went back to Stuttenden, elated to have met up with Peattie but depressed with the case.

Chapter Eight

Callery decided to get tough with them all. He went back to pin Everard Hayes down about his movements the day of the murder. Hayes had an alibi, but Callery wanted proof of it.

'I was teaching,' he answered with a sigh. 'I did what I do every day of every term, I *taught*.'

'All day?'

'Yes, all day – and it felt like it. Preparing utterly bored and uninterested teenagers for their mocks is not a rewarding process.' Hayes reached for the glass on the papers strewing his desk, drained it and poured in a generous refill of whisky. He closed his eyes and sighed. 'They don't want to learn because they know they don't need to, most of them.'

'You mean their parents are rich enough to cushion any failure, get them a good job somewhere anyway?' Callery hated posh people even more.

Everard Hayes opened his tired eyes and gestured his glass towards Callery in agreement. 'Exactly. Maybe there are one or two I get through to, eventually – but not many.'

Callery sighed too, sharing the cynicism and disillusion. 'I suppose your day can be corroborated by other members of staff?'

'Yes yes yes, I'll give you a list of who I had teaching next door to me, who I had coffee with mid-morning, who I lunched with – god, you can ask all the sodding pupils themselves, surely!'

'I will. And your evening?'

' I was in my study marking and sorting out the next day's lessons. Then I went to the pub for supper – plenty of witnesses there too – and went home. I caught the end of some old film on ITV and then went to bed. No witness to that, unfortunately.'

'What was the film?'

'Can't remember.'

'How do you know it was old?'

'There was time to read the credits. Look, is that it? You've enough information to know that I was here, at Stutters, the whole of the day in question. Can I be crossed off your no doubt long list of suspects?'

Callery muttered an 'I suppose so' and left. He heard more whisky being poured into Hayes's glass as he closed the door. God they drank in this place.

Next stop Orlando Fisham. Next door but one, in fact. Fisham was at the sink in a corner of the Art Room, scrubbing at a handful of brushes. He groaned when he saw Callery.

'What *now?* I told you all I know. This could be classed as harassment, I could make an official complaint to the board of governors, do you realise that?' Fisham was trying to look in charge and affronted, but he just came across as scared and tetchy. Like all of the teachers. For a very comfortable, privileged position on the staff of a wealthy institution there was a lot of insecure, unhappy people in such a beautiful building. Hayes, Fisham now, Perry even though she was in charge, Moxey at the other end of the scale – what was the matter with them all?

'Won't take long, Mr Fisham, I can see you're busy.' Callery hoped his sarcasm at seeing Fisham bothering to clean a clutch of stained sticks with such seeming care got through. 'I'd just like to verify your exact movements on the day of Ms Torbet's murder.'

Orlando Fisham gulped, turned the running tap off and tossed the brushes onto the paint-splattered worktop. So much for careful cleaning. He wiped his hands on his still white overall and faced Callery – more sighing, just like all the others.

'I had classes all morning, I had lunch in the canteen with at least three other members of staff who can confirm that, I was in here for the early part of the afternoon preparing an art history talk to my select group of students – the ones who truly want to pursue a career in my own chosen field, and then' – Fisham faltered, grabbed a dirty cloth and wiped already dry taps with it – 'and then I, I— well, I did things in here.' He gulped again and looked at Caller with bulgy eyes.

'What things?' Callery stared back.

More pointless wiping. 'Well, planning, I sat at my desk here and planned – classes. We have to plan ahead, we don't just teach off the cuff, you know.' Fisham managed a weak smile, stopped wiping and gulped with more confidence now. 'And when I left – why, I bumped into one of the teaching assistants who's helping in the Science Podule, she'll tell you she saw me' – Fisham was whizzing now, sure of his ground and happy to talk – 'Yes, sweet little thing, mad about nuclear fission or some such madness, we said hallo, I walked on, went to the staff room and met various colleagues – I can give you a list of at least four – had some much-needed tea, then absolutely rushed to get a train. To Kings Cross, thence to Edinburgh for a weekend with my sister and her husband.' Fisham finished in triumph.

Callery didn't take great pleasure in what he did next, but it was quite enjoyable.

'You're quite right, Mr Fisham,' he said. 'We've already been able to verify that those indeed were your movements on the Thursday of the week in question.'

'Yes? And?'

'Trouble is, Jeanne Torbet was killed on the Friday.'

'Ah. Oh. Well— well, I was in Edinburgh, as I just explained, I was with my sister – well, not actually with her, she was out, at work, she's a director – she's very involved with the festival. In fact it's a bit mad that I go up there then, she's always out and her husband, he works all hours as something in local politics, I'm— I was on my own, I can't actually—' The verifying ran aground and Orlando Fisham just stared.

'So where were you on the day in question?'

'In Scotland. On my own.'

'Okay, Mr Fisham, that's fine for now. If there is anybody or anyway you could confirm your presence in Edinburgh on that date we'd be very grateful.' Callery gave a slick smile and Fisham snatched at it.

'Of course! Yes! I must have been out – well I was, I did, I was out and about during the day, these smarty-arsed tenements are beautiful places to live in now, but they're still a bit claustrophobic to be stuck in all day long! I did, I did go out, I'll dig out some receipts for where I had coffee or whatever, I will.'

'Great.' Callery left. The tap was turned back on; more desperate cleaning, he supposed. He was sure there was a muffled groan amongst the scrubbing.

Adam Thicklow was next. Still mucking about gardening, Callery thought, he's got the Monty Don shirt but not the get-down dirty fingernails, this bloke just empties bags, he doesn't really get to grips with earth.

'Your movements, Mr Thicklow, on the day that Jeanne Torbet died.'

'Pardon?'

'Where were you, on the day of the murder?'

'Here. I'm always here. I work here in this garden, I come and do what I have to and then I leave. I'm no teacher, with classes and meetings and all that rubbish.'

'Yes, but what exactly were you doing in this garden on that day?'

Thicklow shrugged. 'Got here, left my jacket in the glasshouse, came out and did a lot of digging, had a chat with one of Sandra's girls when she came to get stuff for the school lunch, had me own, worked some more, went home – went to the pub on the way home. I don't have anything to do with the school, I never had anything to do with that French woman, I told you that before – why would I have a reason to bump her off?'

It was the same thing, Callery thought. An explanation, lots of reasonable words that could be proved. Like Fisham. Except that Fisham himself changed his version; would Thicklow? Did he need to?

'Can anyone corroborate that?'

'Nope.'

'You don't mind not being able to prove that you weren't on a ferry that day, that you didn't strangle Jeanne Torbet to death in the middle of the English Channel?'

'No.'

'You don't mind or can't prove it?'

'Both. I can answer both. You want to come into the glasshouse for a cuppa?'

Actually Callery did, so he did. It was the best cup of tea he'd had since he'd started this bloody enquiry; an old tin kettle, brewed until proper boiling, tea leaves not bags, a slop of milk into a cracked mug, sitting on a pile of compost sacks, dead comfortable.

'I'm shagging Lucy Makepeace, okay? I was here in the morning, but in the afternoon I wasn't doing my job, I was— I was in Manchester, with her. In her hotel room.'

'Right. In a… shall we say, personal capacity.'

'Yeah.'

'And she'll back that up?'

'She'd better. If I'm in the shit she's in it with me.'

'That's fine, Mr Thicklow. I don't think we need anything further from you at the moment. Now I need to confirm this with Ms Makepeace.'

Callery did; he saw the sweetness fall from Lucy Makepeace's face and leave a look of wary anger, as if a pretty curtain had been swept aside to reveal an ugly iron door.

'Adam Thicklow said that?' she asked challengingly.

'Yes,' said Callery. 'Do you agree with that statement?'

There was silence for a moment – no, not silence. Nothing was said but the whirring of Makepeace's brain as she decided what to say *was* almost audible.

'I do. We are. It's— it's nothing serious, just a fun relationship that neither of us wants anything more from. And it's still an alibi, so I really don't see why this is relevant to—'

'Oh you're quite right, Ms Makepeace, this isn't about that, I just need to corroborate Mr Thicklow's story. Tidy up loose ends.'

'Well I hope this particular very private matter has been tidied up enough for you.' A smile was back, but with no sweetness to it. Callery ended the interview; he didn't think he'd be having another superb lunch in Stutters' refectory any time soon.

****

And then bloody hell, two days later a haggard-looking Fisham asked to see Callery and recanted.

'I wasn't in Edinburgh. I was in Rye with— with Ms Perry. We're— we're in a relationship.'

Not anymore, thought Callery. Once she knows you've spilled the beans she'll do a neat bit of redacting and leave you high and dry, mate.

'That isn't of interest to our enquiry, Mr Fisham,' Callery said smoothly. 'Just a completely truthful account of your movements on the day in question, that's all. Rye then, not Edinburgh?'

'Yes,' Fisham said eagerly. 'You see, it's serious— I mean, Aniska – Ms Perry and I – we're committed, well, it's not just a stupid sex thing you understand, I— I find her deeply honourable and fascinating and she, well I think she feels the same, we're both on the same intellectual plane—'

'Look I just need to know, will Perry back you up that you were with her on the day that Jeanne Torbet was killed?'

'Yes, I'm sure she will. I hope so.' The gulping came back.

'Right, then if she does you're in the clear. Thank you for your… belated honesty, Mr Fisham.' Callery pretended to have to look at his notes. Fisham slunk out.

Callery got to Sutters the following morning, bolstered by a huge full English thanks to the lovely young chap who managed The Haunted Chimney. Sozzy – real name Samuel, but he disowned it in the first three minutes of conversation over pouring excellent coffee. Sozzy said he was Turkish and nobody, nobody left anywhere he worked without feeling as if they'd never eat again – unless they went to Sozzy's mother-in-law's house for lunch. Callery just gave in and ate eight fried eggs, six rashers of bacon, four sausages, ten mushrooms, a pile of baked beans, five tomatoes and four slices of fried bread, then he had a top-up of more bacon and fried bread. Two pots of tea, then a slice or three of more toast and marmalade. Callery was so happy, he almost forgot that he was mired in a case he hadn't solved and didn't look as though he would. Bloody good sausages

It was all closing in. fewer suspects, more reason to close in on the likely one. But then there was another murder.

Chapter Nine

It was lunchtime once more at Stutters. The students exploded into the refectory, stumbling and shouting, youth as powerful and necessary as the electricity running the lighting or the gas in the kitchen. This was surging through the oversized ovens cooking food that wouldn't have been turned down for an EU meeting. The school provided the kitchen equipment to cook the food, the employees to create it; the students supplied the hormonal energy to crave it, consume it. Moneyed need funded top-class supplies, the perfect business model.

The moussaka was a recipe franchised from television's latest celebrity chef, the grilled halloumi alternative accompanied by three different colourful and delicious-looking salads. The water, one of the young women serving explained to Callery, was bottled at source on a private island in the Scottish Hebrides which was owned by the Head Girl's stepfather. A woodland berry compote wasn't the only dessert on offer; chocolate cheesecake was also available, supplied by the company owned by a sixth former's parents, who insisted that their son had a clinically confirmed need for rich desserts due to a glandular condition. They had named him Prospero, after their first date at Stratford-Upon-Avon. The rest of Prospero's class called him Fatty.

Sandra Moxey loomed, checking on the preparations. It was all going smoothly, predictably. Which was perhaps because Lucy Makepeace had put in an appearance; this was because a new version of the usual fish pie was being tested for next week's menu; smoked megrim, not haddock. Sandra Moxey had overseen the production of a trial dish and Lucy Makepeace was here to try it out with her. They went into Moxey's so-called office, a small, windowless space behind the store room. Sandra Moxey opened the huge fridge that almost filled the cramped room and took out two plastic containers.

'These'll only take a few minutes in the microwave—'

Just then a young woman in white overalls stained with vivid purple berry juice stuck her head around the door.

'Sorry, Sandra, there's a phone call for you in the main kitchen – bloke wants to know about Friday's delivery of flour, says the order doesn't look right.'

Sandra Moxey tutted loudly, swore quietly and looked at Makepeace.

'I'll 'ave to take this, my orders is never not perfect—'

'Don't worry Sandra – here, give me those; I'll put them in the microwave and pour us some water, go.'

Moxey left but came back after a couple of minutes and slumped into her chair.

They started to eat in silence. Makepeace was considering the food, but the silence made Moxey sulk.

'I dun my best,' she said sullenly after a couple of generous mouthfuls.

'And you've done brilliantly,' said Lucy, scooping at a small forkful of fish and potato mixed with cheese sauce and herbs; her usual lunch consisted of a rice cake smeared with low-fat hummus and half a tomato. 'Honestly, it's right up to standard. Sandra, this can go straight on the menu, I've no compunction about—'

Lucy Makepeace had no compunction about anything, after that. She choked on the next forkful, her eyes bulged, her throat contracted, she regurgitated the only just eaten fish pie, jolted violently in her chair and then fell face down on the table.

Sandra Moxey stared at her and shovelled another very loaded forkful into her own gob, then swallowed easily. What was going on? Makepeace had just said the meal was okay – more than okay, yet now she was doing all this showing off about spewing it out and fainting. Eh?

Then Sandra Moxey suddenly looked weird. She didn't choke, she didn't vomit, she didn't jolt. She groaned, spat out the remains of megrim and whatever else was in her mouth and slid to the floor.

Outside in the refectory sexual hormones had whirled around, food had been thrown as much as it had been eaten, but youth and wealth had triumphed; the students stumbled out the same way they'd come in. Kitchen staff moved in to clear the mess. The police moved in to deal with the one in Moxey's office.

****

Callery sighed, looked at Moxey's body slumped on the table. This was a dead body; Makepeace's still breathing one had been rushed to hospital and was, apparently, going to be all right. The rest of the plate containing the fish pie was in front of Moxey's fallen head. There was a lot of it left and it looked very good; the pie, not the head. Callery cursed the fact that this seemingly very tasty and probably still warm dish would have to be sealed and sent to forensics whilst he would have to put up with five bags of crisps from a machine somewhere.

He dealt with the crime scene, the body was removed, SOCO took over and the incident was added to the enquiry. Callery knew he'd never get to Calais now; he was doomed to be solving – huh, that would be good! – cases in England, bolting down food whenever he could, never being able to escape and be somebody who travelled to eat, ate, gloried in eating and never had to bother with people – dead ones or alive ones – much again. Callery wanted to be a hermit who had three meals a day at a restaurant just outside the forest where he had his lair.

He made himself think. An attempt had been made to kill two more members of staff at the same prestigious institution, three murders could never be a coincidence and neither was the two that had actually happened; there must be a connection. Torbet; a teacher, loved by some of her students but hated by her peers. Moxey, one of the catering team, disliked by everybody. Makepeace, who didn't seem to have a difficult relationship with anyone else. No, but she did have a furtive relationship with Adam Thicklow. Food had been poisoned and left in Moxey's personal fridge. Which was in her office in the kitchen complex. Where nine other women worked, every day. Where Lucy Makepeace ruled. Where suppliers visited, regularly. Where other people just popped in, like… like Adam Thicklow. Callery had bumped into him that day – only the other day. Thicklow had claimed he was there to cadge a teabag, had run out of his own. Or had that been a cover and he'd nipped into Moxey's office when he knew she'd be shouting at her minions in the kitchen, preparing lunch? So that he had a few crucial moments to add poison to the personal meal portions he knew Moxey kept for herself? This was promising, but it took Callery back to another why – *why* would Thicklow want to kill Sandra Moxey? Or was that just a diversion, include the detested Moxey but the person really meant to die was Makepeace? Had Makepeace tried to end the relationship – she'd seemed pretty offhand about it when he'd spoken to her – and Thicklow wanted revenge?

****

Callery spoke, yet again, with Perry. The reluctance to do this, on both sides, hung in the air like a bad smell. But he had to probe more about the elusive Torbet; everybody had a view about her, but no real knowledge.

Anishka Perry was lying on the floor of her office; not dead, thank god. Callery glanced back through the open door at Lou, who nodded as if to say it's fine, go in. Perry lay still and flat, her hands pressed against the floor, eyes open and staring at the ceiling.

'I'm meditating. What do you want?'

'And I'm investigating. Sorry, I won't keep you long. I just need some more of your incisive thoughts about Jeanne Torbet.'

The bit of flattery didn't work. 'Oh god, how much longer do I need to talk about her? Why can't you just find her killer, Callery?'

A sliver of a smile crossed Perry's face, as if she liked the alliteration and using Callery's name without his title. Right.

'There have now been two murders connected with this school, Ms Perry – can you sit up and give me the information I need? The sooner you do that, the sooner I'll be out of your office. The sooner I find the killer the better it will be for the reputation of this school. Stuttenden will stop feeding the media with the blood it craves and the media will stop harassing us all.'

That hit home. It was true, photographers from the global press and TV had been kept to slinking around outside the exotic but impenetrable school gates (gift of a Saudi prince's parents who appreciated the rules being relaxed enough for him to gain one A-level in Basic Art). But social media was having orgasms about all the theories and rumours. Perry got up, put her vertiginous heels back on and sat behind her desk.

'What exactly do you want to know now?'

'Just more – a bit more. Just tell me more about Torbet's students – the close ones.'

'Okay. Yes, Madame Torbet's clique, her little group of admirers; Chloe and Tallulah and Bethany and Isabeau – *another* Chloe… Emma, Venus-Hepzibah – her mother used to be married to a rock star – Olivia, Adaego/07 – oh yes, that's Venus's sister when the mother divorced the rock star and married a pop star – goodness me, the girls that have flowed through here. I can't possibly remember every single one of them.' Anishka Perry seemed to run aground, recalling the parentage of so many of her students.

'And how admiring were these students?'

'Well, all teachers can have that, thinking *their* teacher's the most wonderful human being ever. It stops as soon as the girls start properly meeting boys.'

'Right, boys,' Callery said, edging nearer to what he was after. 'Were there any of the male pupils who— who might have felt like that about Ms Torbet?'

'You mean were there any boys who fancied her?'

'Well— yes.'

'Are you asking me if Jeanne Torbet had a sexual relationship with one of our male students?'

'Yes.'

'No. I told you all this the first time. Torbet was – how can I describe it – she was immune to human contact, in a way. She had this imperviousness to friendship. She even kept me at arm's length.'

Callery could imagine that most people would want to keep this hard-edged woman at a distance. She looked as though she never cried, ever.

****

It was a quiet pause in the garden at Stuttenden school. Mid-afternoon, mid-September. Adam Thicklow sat outside his shed on his favourite pile of old sacks with yet another cuppa. What a lovely moment; good work done, birds chatting, that wonderful smell of the earth. Callery had done him an injustice; Thicklow genuinely felt proud of what he achieved in the gardens.

As he sipped he looked out over the huge stretch of immaculate grass he'd cut that morning, ready for the parents' evening in a few hours. These occasions at Stutters weren't like they were in any ordinary school; rushed, awkward collisions of embarrassed mothers and fathers with jaded teachers. Platitudes exchanged, concerns aired on both sides then left undealt with. A Stuttenden evening was delightful; a glass of the finest champagne in the gracious entrance hall before a cursory meeting with the teacher of the parents' choice (so the one who'd deliver the best report). Then an elegant trip across the lawn to sit and listen to a marvellously insightful and witty speech from the Head (not too long), which presaged some exquisite chamber music from the best young professional players available (not too long). And the climax of the evening; dinner in the refectory, like-minded people, all wealthy, all well-connected, all of the same political persuasion, all revelling in being dressed up, eating and drinking the best food and wines available (for as long as possible).

Those few hours passed. Parents fell out of high-priced cars and made their classily-dressed way across the perfect lawn for a wonderful evening. The flawless life they'd worked hard for was laid out in front of them; the best education that money could buy as the setting for superb food and wine and culture (mustn't forget that) amongst others who were exactly the same. Wealth totally vindicated, effort gloriously justified.

The lawn was now like a meadow, studded with figures in black or a variety of vivid colours; there wasn't a dress or suit label in the whole garden that hadn't commanded a price tag of less than a thousand pounds (tax-deductible). Champagne was poured, swallowed, the canapés toyed with. The concert was appropriately applauded. Stupid but good-looking children were paraded, unprepossessing but intelligent ones were equally showed-off. Later, the dutiful stuff done, the real fun would start in the refectory. Ties would be loosened, jokes made, awful remarks about poor people guffawed at, the kids that cost all this money packed off home to bed. Adam Thicklow wasn't ever included in the line-up of school personnel to be presented, but he was watching from his shed. He went inside and poured himself a glass of whisky from the secret bottle hidden behind a wholesaler's seed catalogue. Then he sat outside, enjoying the Brahms and Schubert from a distance. The music didn't really calm him though; now he was worried, seriously worried. Once more, Thicklow thought. I want to get out of this – I'll do it once more and then I'm out. He sipped, as with the tea. But unlike the comforting, familiar cuppa, this first swallow of the whisky was his last.

****

Callery sighed. He felt like any of the teachers in this awful place, always sighing and cynical. But he had a right to be like that, didn't he? Another murder for god's sake, the third – and he hadn't even solved the first one. Thicklow's body had been found, slumped over some sacks in his shed, by a couple of pupils hoping it would be empty so they could have a pleasant time with some top-quality dope. A perfunctory analysis showed he'd been poisoned by the same toxin that had done for Moxey and nearly for Makepeace.

Torbet, Moxey, Thicklow – what was the link? Was there one? Had to be, of course – you don't get more than one unnatural death in the same place without a connection – first detective rule in the notebook. Okay, Torbet wasn't liked, neither was Moxey – but Thicklow wasn't resented by anybody, he was a harmless, powerless gardener. Or was he? Thicklow's whole background would have to be gone into now.

Callery demanded yet another meeting with Anishka Perry. She refused. He insisted. He finally got into her office for an absolute limit of ten minutes, he was told.

'Ms Perry, there have now been three deaths connected with your school,' Callery started with a confidence he'd learned in detective school, but had never become genuine. Anishka Perry knew it, instinctively.

'You haven't solved the first yet – and now two more, as you so intelligently point out.' The contempt in the word intelligent was like a shot of venom from the most lethal snake David Attenborough had ever been filmed staring at from a very safe distance. Callery now had three murders to solve; he was failing, like one of Perry's worst, least fee-paying pupils.

'Yes. I have a strong suspicion that the three are connected. The solution to them all is here, Ms Perry, I'm afraid.'

'You should be afraid, detective Callery. To sort of paraphrase Oscar Wilde, three bodies looks like gross carelessness.' She stared at him, invincible. Callery stared back.

'I'm not scared, Ms Perry – I'm tired. Tired of too much crime and no help – from you or your staff. Adam Thicklow didn't help me much, neither did Sandra Moxey before him. If she'd been more open with our enquiries she might not have been killed, if he had he might not have died.'

'You've omitted Jeanne Torbet; if you'd found her murderer the other two wouldn't have happened, would they?'

Callery nearly started gulping like Orlando Fisham, but didn't let it get a grip. 'We're on the case. With more assistance from you all here – from you particularly as the person in charge of this organisation—'

Anishka Perry shuffled some papers on her desk, looked up at Callery and flicked a gorgeous eyebrow upwards. 'I'll give you all the information you need. I will also protect to the hilt my people. I have the fullest confidence in whoever works for me and will not hesitate to defend every one of us against any unjust accusation, be it instigated by any official body.'

'Look, everyone I've spoken to hated Jeanne Torbet. Sandra Moxey wasn't liked. I've interviewed enough of your staff to know how much office relationships are going on – you haven't got a perfect staff, Ms Perry, stop pretending you have. Why don't people like each other?'

Callery had thrown in the need to explain, but of course it was up to him, not her, to sort it all out. He wasn't getting anywhere and Perry knew it.

Chapter Ten

He walked into the Haunted Chimney to order a pint and who should pop up behind the bar but Lisa Choke.

'Shouldn't you be in the shop?' Callery asked, pointing at the pump for a very decent local beer that he'd drunk the last time he was there. Lisa smiled and started pulling.

'This is my other job – can't make a livin' only sellin' posh fruit and veg, can I? You want a pasty with this, sausage roll, Scotch Egg?'

'Yes please.'

Lisa Choke looked perplexed for a moment, then realised that Callery meant it, laughed and got him a plate with all three on it. 'That lot'll still cost you less than one of the shop's paninis,' she whispered with another artless grin.

Callery wanted to air one of his many grievances and tell her that panini was a plural word already and didn't need the s, but didn't. He liked Lisa. She was refreshingly free from the rampant ambition and bile he met with at Stutters. He hoped she'd stay chatting; luckily nobody else came in for a bit so she could. And did.

'Three murders now, Mr. Policeman – not good, is it?'

Callery swallowed a big gulpful of beer and shook his head.

'Not surprised you're gettin' nowhere,' said Lisa. 'Closed in lot in that school. You're not posh enough for any of them to let you know what really goes on.'

'What does go on?'

Lisa smiled again. 'Well… buy me a Cointreau and I might tell you.'

'Of course – are you allowed to drink on duty? I'm not.'

'I finish in ten minutes; the boss knows when he's got good staff.'

Lisa Choke poured herself an enormous glass of the orange liqueur, took a good swig and leant one arm on the bar. 'Thanks.'

'My pleasure.' Callery and Lisa raised their glasses to each other. He waited. After another generous mouthful Lisa spoke.

'We-ell... everybody there – all of 'em, the Head, teachers, kids, their parents – are all insane about showing off how successful they are and paranoid because they're not as good as they pretend to be.'

'I can see that,' said Callery. 'But why are they all so obsessed? They *are* successful people, aren't they? Anishka Perry, some of the teachers, a lot of the pupils, they're privileged, sure to succeed. The parents; they're mostly rolling in it, what's their problem?'

'The school's in the shit, money-wise. It's on the verge of collapse, with huge debts.'

Callery had thought Lisa was going to be helpful, but now it seemed she might just be elevating nasty gossip into shocking facts. 'Now how do you know that?' he said sceptically.

Lisa did one of her conspiratorial leanings close to him and dropped her voice. 'Because my dad's ex-brother-in-law works for the school's accountancy firm. He told my dad the school was on the skids ages ago. He said there's goin' to be trouble, big trouble before it goes belly up, with them all tryin' to save their skins and blame it on somebody else. He said he wouldn't be surprised if there was unexplained death – well now there is, isn't there?'

'We don't have the killer or killers yet, no,' said Callery. 'But the deaths are explained; strangling and poison.'

Lisa shook her head impatiently. 'No no, I don't mean how it was done. My dad's ex-brother-in-law meant why it was done. People would be bumped off because of *what they knew.*'

'And what exactly did they know? Come on Lisa, finish that and I'll buy you another – but only if you give me a second pint too and give me more than titillating rumour.'

Lisa emptied her glass and gave it a voluptuous refill, then replenished Callery's. She wasn't sure what titillating meant but genuinely wanted to help this gangling, nice detective.

'Okay. Cheers. Perry and the governors are all on the fiddle, always have been. Money's been creamed off from the start, it was the whole reason the school was opened. My dad's ex-brother-in-law reckons his boss is in on it – his house is far too grand for somebody with a little accountant's in Stuttenden – three Mercedes and a Porsche in that family! My dad's ex-brother-in-law says the only reason he hasn't gone to the police with what he knows is cos he's scared he'll get killed too. And he was right, wasn't he? I mean, look what's happened; three murders – well, that must mean three people did start sayin' what they'd found out and they got killed because of it!'

'Why on earth didn't you tell me all this before?' said Callery. Lisa looked sheepish. 'Well, it's family stuff, isn't it? 'Spose I felt guilty tellin' you before.'

'How come now?'

'One murder's a bit sort of excitin',' she explained, the sheepish look still there. 'But three – well that's no joke, is it?'

'You're dead right about that,' Callery said ruefully. 'What's this ex-brother-in-law's name? Why don't you use it?' Lisa grinned again, but a bit sheepishly this time.

'Cos he's bad news. My dad's not supposed to be talkin' to him. Our family and his fell out, big time.'

'May I ask why?'

'My dad's ex-brother-in-law, he was married to my dad's sister. Divorced a while ago now. She was a right bitch, stirred up trouble no end between my mum and all of us – but she knew what was goin' on at the school alright, what she told my dad's ex-brother-in-law while they were still married, that was what started him lookin' into what was goin' on at the accountant's. And now she's paid the price for knowin' what she did!' Lisa ended triumphantly.

'Your dad's ex-brother-in-law's wife is one of the victims?' Callery said, taken aback. 'Who?'

Lisa Choke finished her drink and finished her tale. 'Sandra Moxey.'

Callery nearly spat out the last of his pint. 'Moxey was your aunt? Christ Lisa, there's so much you've held out on me about!'

Lisa Choke shrunk into her shoulders and looked penitent. 'Sorry, 'spose I should've. That school, it's so closed off even though it's such a big part of this village – oh I dunno, I just felt that these murders weren't to do with us ordinary folk. Sorry!'

Callery fancied another pint but resisted. His head was still relatively clear and he wanted to get back to his room and pore over this latest information. Fundamental corruption at Stuttenden. Sandra Moxey: worked at the school, suspected what was going on, told her then husband who corroborated it with his own surreptitious enquiries at his place of work. Sandra Moxey: a blackmailer. Who probably finally tried to extort money from the wrong person because of what she knew and was killed as a result. Was Jeanne Torbet murdered for the same reason? Disliked, secretive, could have been trying blackmail as well and suffered the same fate as Moxey. Adam Thicklow? Callery couldn't see him as a blackmailer; did he accidentally stumble across some knowledge he shouldn't have? Accidentally see something he shouldn't? And had to go too?

It was all getting too complicated – and Callery knew from experience that murder was never complicated. Somebody wanted somebody else dead. And if someone else knew anything incriminating they had to be murdered too. Three deaths now; three terrible crimes and Callery had nobody to pin them on. He felt tricked; Moxey working on the ferries had led him to think that would solve Torbet's death – but then Moxey was killed and Thicklow seemed to be implicated – and then *he* was bumped off. It seemed to be a pattern, but one designed only to fool him. He tried to think straight. Who had hated Torbet, Moxey and Thicklow so much – or feared them so much – that they had to be murdered? Callery had a huge breakfast – big even for him, he needed the comfort – and plunged into his notes on the case.

Jeanne Torbet had been strangled. Sandra Moxey and Adam Thicklow had been poisoned, the same way. Forensics had reported that the substance used had been weedkiller – from the same source, Thicklow's shed. But too late for Callery to be able to interview Thicklow again, this time as a definite murder suspect – if not for Torbet, at least for Moxey. Who wanted Torbet dead enough to follow her onto a ferry – or arrange to meet her on it? And wanted Moxey and Thicklow dead enough to kill them in situ? Were the three victims in league against the killer to stop blackmail? Had they been involved in some appalling sexual thing that Torbet had discovered? Had it been the four of them doing something unspeakable, Torbet had wanted out so she had to be silenced to save the others, then they turned on each other – who'd be next? Callery's head was spinning – should he just wait for one more murder and then he'd have the last one left as the guilty? Jesus, what a job; to hope for more violent death in order to hand in a good report…

****

Callery requested one more meeting with Perry; he was granted five minutes of her precious time after assembly the following morning. This time he had ammunition.

'Speak quickly, Mr Callery,' Perry said, swiping off her vertiginous heels for some stylish flats and clamping herself in the chair behind her huge desk. 'I have three meetings before eleven o'clock and then need to go to London for a working lunch with a potential investor.'

'Investor?' said Callery, squatting in a useless chair by the door and flicking through his notes. 'In what?'

Anishka Perry looked surprised. 'In the school of course, what else? Charming man, the prince. A friend of the American and the Russian presidents, his wealth paves many ways to success for many businesses. And what is education but a business – the business of grooming for wealth and power?' Perry smiled as if she'd just eaten a chunk of luxury chocolate.

Callery didn't bother replying that he though education meant being taught to read and write, coughed and hunched over in the ridiculous chair.

'I have to ask you a… delicate question, Ms Perry,' he said.

'Well ask, we've already wasted three minutes.'

'Were you at a hotel in Rye with Orlando Fisham on the day of Jeanne Torbet's murder?'

Anishka Perry stared at Callery as if he'd asked her if she'd ever considered a job at a school in Jaywick.

'Where? She snorted.

'Rye. Nice place, apparently. Cobbled streets, good tea rooms and restaurants. Had a lot of smuggling, I believe—'

'I was not in Rye or anywhere else with Mr Fisham! Where on earth did you get the idea that I could have been?' Anishka Perry was now drumming her perfectly-manicured nails on her desk as if she was playing a piano. Very fast.

'Are you sure? Mr Fisham is.'

Perry blinked a bit. Good sign. 'He's mistaken.'

'He gave me this receipt—' Callery handed it over. 'Two people, one room – best en suite – lunch and dinner. Paid by you, I believe.'

More blinking, and the piano playing had stopped. 'It has nothing to do with me.'

Callery was enjoying this; Anishka Perry would have to react better when she was pressed on BBC's Question Time.

'It was paid with your bank card. We checked.'

Perry capitulated. A pacific smile flashed on to her face. 'Okay,' she said, sitting back in her chair. 'Oh dear, how our minor peccadilloes catch up with us. Yes, I did spend that night with – Orlando in Rye. It… it was a brief liaison, a diversion from the pressures of work for both of us. I may be a dynamic leader with, I'm not afraid to say, great ambition, but I am still a woman, Mr Callery. And, I hope, an attractive one…'

She looked at Callery and he realised that she was being seductive, trying to make him understand how Rye with Fisham happened. He felt like a fifth-former transfixed by the glare of a classmate's sex-starved parent. He wanted out of this room.

'Right,' he said, wrenching himself out of his chair. 'You admit that this receipt is proof of your stay with Orlando Fisham on the Friday that Jeanne Torbet was killed?' He took the incriminating slip back.

'Yes.' The seductive smile had gone and the flat shoes were coming off. 'I'll corroborate it in any way you want. Just— just be diplomatic about it, will you?' The teetering heels were back on and Anishka Perry showed Callery to the door.

'Mr Fisham was as co-operative as yourself; I appreciate it,' he said as he left.

'Mr Fisham?' said Perry in her usual brittle way. 'I'm so glad – I wouldn't like him to leave the school with any ambiguity clouding his reputation.'

****

Now for Hayes. Callery passed the Science Park on his way to the Expression Pod and came across a young woman mopping the corridor. She smiled at him, then seemed to want to speak.

'You want to talk to Ms Bianchi? About this murder?' The young woman seemed willing to help, not wary and defensive.

'Yes. I'm just double-checking the teachers' whereabouts on the day of the killing – I know Ms Bianchi herself is in the clear, at some conference in Geneva; that was confirmed early on in my enquiries.'

'I know, we all know. The staff – they've all gone on about where they were, ordinary day, usual lessons and all that. Bianchi – she was abroad, left on the Tuesday and wasn't back until Sunday.' The young woman smiled and relaxed a bit, leaning on her mop as if she was talking over the garden fence. 'She's Italian – my dad's from Naples, she and me – well, we like having a chat in Italian sometimes. She's nice.'

Callery relaxed for a moment too; a normal person. 'Your English is brilliant.'

'Oh, I was born in Crystal Palace! But you know, you grow up and get taught your background – so did Sylvia – sorry, Ms Bianchi. Except she was born in Italy, in Rome.'

'It must be nice for you to have that in common.'

'Yeah, it is… but if you already know that the Expression Pod was closed, why do you need to check again?'

'Pardon?'

'Well, no teaching was going on here for any of them, not that day.'

Callery felt he was near something. 'Why not?'

'There was a fire alarm. Classes stopped. We all went out onto the playing field and thought we'd be back in after a bit, but apparently something had gone wrong with the system, not just the blip they all get every so often – too often if you ask me. The alarm company was called in, we had the day off – well, teachers did.'

'And the cleaning staff?'

'We carried on. A big fire starts and it's okay if we're still in the building – what, *we* won't burn to death?'

'So none of the teachers was here that day?'

'No. The other two – Fisham and Hayes – they hadn't come in at all.'

'You mean the whole school?' Callery didn't understand why nobody had mentioned this before.

'No no – each of the blocks has its own system, they're individual. It was only the Pod bit that had a fire alarm. Everywhere else just carried on as usual.'

Callery's brain computed quickly. All the other people that had been checked out at the beginning; they threw up nothing odd because nothing odd happened to them, it was a normal working day, nobody missing. But in this part of the school he'd only had – well, it was only Fisham and Hayes. Fisham had been found out, so was now in the clear. But Hayes – Callery now knew that Hayes had totally lied about what he'd done that Friday.

'You've been very helpful, Ms—?'

The nice smile came back. 'Scarpe. Angelina Scarpe is my name. Ms Shoes. Funny eh, when I'm on my feet all day long?'

Callery smiled back. 'It's a lovely name. Thankyou.'

He bet Ms Shoes cooked some delicious pasta. But now he had to have another go at Everard Hayes; ordinary school day my foot.

****

'Mr Hayes, why did you lie about where you were on the day Jeanne Torbet was killed?'

Hayes froze in the doorway of his classroom, where Callery had accosted him. His hand was on the doorknob; it squeaked as Hayes' hand gripped it as if it was crying out on Hayes' behalf.

'Lie?' he said in a quiet voice.

'Yes,' said Callery in a loud, confident one. 'That Friday wasn't an ordinary one for you at all, was it?'

'Wasn't it?'

'No – there was a fire alarm in this part of the school. It was evacuated and nobody was allowed back in for the rest of the day.'

The doorknob squeaked again.

'Was there?' Hayes swallowed, but it wasn't gin going down this time, it was fear coming up.

'Yes,' said Callery. 'Would you mind telling me where you really were, Mr Hayes?'

'Oh god, nobody said. I came back and nobody told me.'

'Nobody else in the school was aware of the alarm – it was an ordinary day for them. And there wasn't anyone else in this block who could tell you, was there? Fischer, Bianchi and Abreu were away, Fisham's been accounted for – he wasn't here either and Torbet – well, Torbet was on her way to being dead, wasn't she? You were the only other teacher who should have been here on that day.' Callery smiled triumphantly. 'Where were you?'

'I— I was with her.'

'Her? Who?'

'Jeanne Torbet. I was— I was on the same ferry.'

Callery gaped. Had he finally got the killer of Torbet?'

'Mr Hayes, I think you need to let go of that door handle and come with me so that we can talk.'

Callery took Everard Hayes into an empty office.

'I have to warn you, Mr Hayes, that unless you can provide a convincing explanation of your presence on board the ship where the killing of Jeanne Torbet took place, I may have to charge you.'

Hayes slumped in his chair, defeated. Was this it, Callery thought. Have I got the murderer of maybe three people?

'I can explain; it won't be very edifying, but it's the truth.' Hayes sighed heavily and sat up. 'Okay. I was on that boat to go to Calais for the day. It was a complete coincidence that Jeanne Torbet was there too; I was horrified when I caught sight of her – I saw her go into the first class lounge and made sure I kept well away from it. I assumed she was going back to France for good, having left the school.'

'Why were you travelling?'

'I— I had arranged to meet somebody. A young man from Wimereux. We met online. We were going to have lunch. I— I'm a lonely man, Inspector Callery.'

'But you never got to France; none of us did.'

'No.' Hayes sighed again, sadly. 'I doubt that it would have been a success, anyway. He looked very handsome on the website; tall and slim, lots of dark curly hair and a gorgeous smile. In real life he's probably a fat lout with bad skin. His photo was a fake, I expect; I know mine was.'

'You didn't kill Jeanne Torbet? Did you kill Sandra Moxey and Adam Thicklow?'

'No to all three. I proved where I was on board and when Torbet was killed – in the passenger lounge the whole time. And my alibis for the other two are genuine, you know that.'

Reluctantly, Callery did. Hayes was definitely in the clear for Moxey and Thicklow's deaths; he'd known that but thought he'd try unnerving Hayes. Now he tackled what had bothered him since Hayes had said he was onboard.

'I didn't see your name on the passenger list. How come? It would have had to be the same as the one on your passport, otherwise you wouldn't have been allowed to board.'

'It is.' Hayes looked as if he didn't care what was revealed now.

'There was no Everard Hayes on that list.'

'There's no Everard Hayes on my passport. It's not my real name.'

'Ah, I see… what is it, Mr— Mr?'

'Hammond. My real name is Eddie Hammond.'

'Does Ms Perry know that?'

'No. Nobody here does. I faked my name to make myself sound more— more intellectual, more erudite. I falsified my references too.'

'More faking. You seem to do a lot of that… Mr Hammond.' Callery wondered if the denial of murder had been faked as well.

'Yes. I did a rather good job, if I may say so. Convinced Perry, anyway. She'd never have employed an average English teacher from a west London comprehensive, but she was keen to snare a private tutor with a first-class degree from Oxford. One with glowing references from a Nigerian diplomat, a Russian oligarch and a Japanese billionaire.'

'But she would have checked them, surely?'

'By emails. Which came to me. It's not hard to do stuff like that – and Perry saw what she wanted to see. The salaries at Stutters – like some of the teachers – aren't what you'd call top level.'

Callery realised that as Hayes had metamorphosed into Hammond his accent had changed. It wasn't clipped and precise, almost camp; now it had the flat, widened pronunciation of Londoners. Hayes would never have used a sloppy word like stuff; but Hammond did. Callery also realised that Hayes/Hammond was probably in the clear for Torbet's murder. Back to square one.

'I've got to admit to something else,' said the now unpatrician Hammond.

'Oh god, what,' said Callery.

'It's okay, it's nothing to do with the killings. I just want to completely clear the decks,'

'What is it?'

Eddie Hammond – well, it was incredible – he was relaxed, honest and innocent, on Callery's side. Totally unlike the wary, deceitful Everard Hayes who Callery had interviewed at the start of the inquiry.

'I had a thing – a brief thing, for me anyway – with Sandra Moxey.'

'And? Has that fact anything to do with any of the murders?'

Hammond shrugged. 'S'pose not. I thought you'd like to know. She – she was good for information. About anything.'

'Like what?'

'Like our wonderful head and Mr Fisham.'

'I know about that. They had a consensually beneficial relationship, shall we say.'

'Oh. Okay. Sandra also said that Torbet was gay. And that her little group of admirers – they were more than that. Well, one of them was.'

'What are you talking about, Mr – Hammond? Or would you like me to go back to addressing you as Mr Hayes?'

'I don't mind.' More shrugging. 'It doesn't matter now, I'm finished here. Jeanne Torbet was in a serious relationship with one particular student.'

'Oh. Right. Who was it?'

'I'm not sure. Sandra wasn't, either. It could have been any of them. Sorry.'

'Not as much as I am.'

Chapter Eleven

Callery prowled the school, poking into the teachers' offices when they weren't there, wandering around the refectory, the classrooms and along the plush corridors once the students and staff had left. He found himself back in Sandra Moxey's tiny office for the fifth time since the murder, looking for something that would help. The scene of crime tape was still draped across the doorway but it sagged now, as if it was tired of being on duty. Callery stepped over it and stood inside, staring round him. Same desk where the death happened, cleaned now of course. Same vast fridge, same microwave, same crap piled up on every forensically-tested surface. He got fed up with looking round, looked up. Shelves that held cookery books, paperwork, catalogues from suppliers went up part of one wall behind Moxey's desk; the top shelf was empty apart from dusty and dirty beer glasses. Callery's gaze went round the room at the same height… and then he saw it. On top of a cupboard he saw the same ancient folders bulging with paid bills that had littered Moxey's desk. They tottered next to her used overalls and piles of what looked like old newspapers. They looked as though they'd all just been shoved up there, redundant but not recycled. Shoved and yet placed; the piles were actually, on more careful examination, deliberately positioned, forming a sort of protecting wall. Protecting what? Callery got a chair, stood on it and peered. From the floor it couldn't be seen, but up here a round lens was visible, poking through the folders, a good view of the room created for it – a security camera. That filmed, in secret. Filmed secret activity. Callery nearly fell off the chair.

****

It was quite straightforward getting the camera removed and what was on it made available to view. There was some tedious stuff with Moxey berating any of her team who'd had the bad luck to be called into her office and a bit of Moxey herself, alone and drunk, staring up at the camera with a full glass in her hand, tearfully confiding into the lens that she was a good girl really, she was only 'tectin' 'erself, it weren't fair, but the key part – the bit that Sandra Moxey would have loved to know she'd captured – was categoric evidence of her own murder. The killer, caught red-handed. Red-suited, as it happened; Lucy Makepeace in one of her customary well-tailored outfits, manicured hands taking two plastic containers from Sandra Moxey and the latter leaving the office, one of her girls in the doorway. Left alone, Makepeace was seen to swiftly put the containers on Moxey's desk, take a small pot from her bag and decant the contents into them – the greater part into the one that was subsequently emptied onto Moxey's plate. She put the containers into the microwave and clicked buttons before calmly pouring bottled water into two glasses and waiting. Moxey returned, the cooked food was taken from the microwave, the food served and ate. Callery knew the rest.

A few hours later he embarked on the formality of charging Lucy Makepeace. His voice ran through the familiar words in a toneless, disinterested way.

'You're under arrest on suspicion of the murders of Sandra Moxey and Adam Thicklow. You don't have to say anything, but it may harm your defence if you don't mention when questioned something which you later rely on in court. Anything you do say will be given in evidence. Do you understand?'

Makepeace was unperturbed. 'And I committed them how?'

'Weedkiller, both times. Threw me off the scent, that did, that was clever of you, Ms Makepeace. One murder that pointed very strongly in the direction of somebody who had easy access to weedkiller – like Adam Thicklow. He was our suspect, I'll admit – until he too died.'

'I was poisoned too, remember! I didn't walk out of that room smiling and triumphant.'

Now Callery did get interested; he could get ready to drop his bombshell.

'You put a miniscule amount in your small portion, far less than what you carefully folded into Sandra Moxey's larger one.'

'When? In front of her eyes? It was her office we were in remember, not mine.'

'She had to leave the office for a few minutes, didn't she?'

'Did she?' Lucy Makepeace shrugged carelessly. 'I forget.'

'Well that's odd, seeing as how she left to take a phone call; one you'd engineered yourself. One made by your lover and your second victim, Mr Thicklow. Those few minutes – timed to the second by you and Thicklow – were all you needed to poison the food, put it in the microwave and then serve it. Thicklow did what he was supposed to – and so did Moxey, innocently eating what you knew would kill her.'

Makepeace snorted. 'Greedy cow, served her right.' She sat back in the hard upright chair she'd been given and crossed her slim legs. If people still smoked the way they used to she'd have lit up a Balkan Sobranie, Callery thought. A pink one, with a gold tip. 'Anyway, this is all supposition, you've got no proof.'

'Oh but we have.' Here it came. 'Didn't know about the camera, did you?

The contemptuous look on Lucy Makepeace's face froze. If she had been smoking she'd have tensed, leaned forward and stubbed the cigarette out with force, thinking wildly as she did it.

'What camera? Where? I know everything that goes on in my department, I never sanctioned Sandra Moxey having a camera installed.'

'No, you didn't. It's a fairly basic one, not expensive; Moxey paid for it to be fitted herself. I guess she just liked spying on whoever came into her office. It's above a pile of newspapers on top of that cabinet opposite her desk. You can't see it from lower down, but it can see everything that goes on. Clever; I only spotted it after a fifth visit. And the footage we got from it shows you indisputably putting poison into the food. The jury'll like watching that.'

Lucy Makepeace was breathing heavily now. She was cornered, like an animal at bay.

'I don't believe you. You're trying to trick me into a confession. I ingested the weedkiller as well, didn't I? Explain that!'

'Like I said, you gave yourself a miniscule amount, enough to make you sick but not kill you.

'I gagged! I choked before Moxey did, I collapsed, you could see that, if you've got this film you're talking about!'

'Exaggeration. And insurance. If Moxey hadn't died it would have seemed as if somebody else had tried to kill both of you.'

Makepeace would by now have been on a third fag. 'Shit.'

'Quite,' said Callery. 'Why did you do it, Ms Makepeace? You earn a very good salary at this school I believe.'

The contemptuous expression came back. 'Kids? You think teaching spoilt kids is a way to make money? Education? Oh no – it's not the young, it's the *old*.' Lucy Makepeace, trapped, was letting all her bile spew out. 'I wanted enough cash to start a chain of classy care homes – good ones, the equivalent of Stuttenden but catering for those who drool, dither and crap themselves rather than those who've grown out of all that for a few decades. Actually it's exactly the same, except the young ones know they're demanding it and the old ones don't.'

'Why didn't you get a business loan, like anyone else?' asked Callery.

Lucy Makepeace laughed nastily. 'I didn't want to. I wanted the ability to be as wealthy as possible, as soon as possible.' She sighed. 'So I— I set up a plan with one of our suppliers – I'll give you all the dirt on him, you should be able to send him away for a few years, he was willing enough.'

'To do what?' Callery knew what was coming though. Good old fraud.

'He falsified invoices, inflated the charges for everything, I had the authority to pay them of course and we split the difference. I have an extremely generous budget for catering, as you might have surmised.'

'And Sandra Moxey found out what you were up to.'

'She did.'

'So Sandra Moxey had to die.'

'She did. She got a good enough idea – and used it.'

'How?'

'I stupidly left my phone in my office one afternoon when I was out. Moxey had a good look at the texts on it and guessed. And started blackmailing me; I couldn't have that.'

'And Adam Thicklow?'

'He was in on it too; fake invoices from the same supplier. It's a big company and my man there charged Adam far more for his orders than was delivered, same trick. I made the mistake of thinking he was cannier and harder than he was, I thought he would want the money as much as I did. Adam was good for coitus on the compost in that shabby old shed of his, but he got boring – and scared. He wanted out and threatened to go to the police. So he had to go too.'

'That was how you got hold of the weedkiller for Moxey?'

'That's what really spooked him. Stealing he could – reluctantly – handle, but when Moxey died he knew it was me and panicked.'

Callery should have felt satisfied, but he didn't. He yearned to ask Lucy Makepeace if she'd murdered Jeanne Torbet as well and be told yes. But he knew her alibi for that was solid; he still hadn't solved everything.

Chapter Twelve

Callery wandered into Lou Shelbourne's office as if he was lost on a beach that wouldn't get to anywhere. It just stretched on, like his enquiries. He had so much information, so many views from so many – possible – suspects, but had nothing definite to rely on, use. Pebbles, not concrete. And then he suddenly came across a point to the wandering.

'Hallo, Mr Detective,' said Lou, looking up from her laptop. 'Called in for a coffee, or is it more formal than that, another of your constant requests to see Ms Perry?'

That's not very nice, Callery thought. The ranks closing again, the nastiness in this school being protected, everybody in it disloyal but loyal at the same time. He decided to be pleasant.

'Coffee yes, thank you, Ms Perry no, not at the moment. I need to step back, consider. I need to be out of, out of—'

'Out of this school? Not literally, but mentally? You must. It's draining, if you teach here, I've realised that. Stuttenden is so well endowed in so many ways, but there's something empty at the heart of it, isn't there? I think that's why Torbet was killed.'

Callery had taken a cup of the excellent coffee poured by Ms Shelbourne from the most sophisticated coffee-making machine available and was sipping gratefully.

'You sound disenchanted. I thought you liked your job.'

'I did. Now I don't. All this wealth and comfort is one thing, the culture here ending in murder is another. I'm leaving at the end of this term; don't tell Perry.'

'Of course. Will you miss it?'

Lou pondered. 'Not really. It's just a job, I'll find another. I can be PA to a Spad any time I want, be in on the next Parliament.'

'How?' Callery suspected what was coming.

'Another uncle.'

'And won't you take anything from Stuttenden?'

'Apart from the high heels and emergency tampons in my desk drawer, you mean? Not much. That's sad, isn't it? Three years of utter slaving to Perry and that's all that's mine in this place.'

'I meant proper memories – come on, young people like you have images of everything, all the time, non-stop. It's your lives, you aren't alive unless it's recorded and can be shown to the world.'

'You sound old and bitter, Mr Detective. You can't be that old, I'm not that young. Go on, how old are you?'

'Thirty-eight.'

'Well I'm thirty-four, so neither of us is addicted to social media, I suspect. I was away from all of that for a while. I lived in India for three years, in a village miles from anywhere.'

'Don't tell me – with yet another uncle.'

'Yep, sorry. Ed, he's a billionaire media mogul – in fact it's sort of real, he's descended from an actual Mogul, historically, can you believe it?

'Yeah, I can,' said Callery wearily. 'How many uncles have you got?'

'Loads. I've got twenty-seven cousins.'

Callery gave up. 'Sorry, I'm asking personal stuff, not relevant.'

Lou Shelbourne laughed, but warmly. 'It doesn't matter. Actually you've reminded me, asking about memories. I must delete a load of my school stuff on my office phone before I leave – nothing dubious, but if I'm off I suppose I should clear it.'

Callery's instincts as a policeman woke up. 'What school stuff?'

'Just daily life, really. You know how American schools used to have year books, where every student was logged with a photo and something about what they're like and going to be? I started trying to do the same thing here, but it was too chaotic to organise, too many kids cleared off too early at the end of term with their parents, teachers agreed to join in but then it all just disintegrated – so I just started filming the kids whenever I could, just bits of them doing whatever – you know, in the corridors between classes, outside after classes. I just wanted to catch them being normal – just being them.'

'Can I see?' said Callery. 'Can you show me?'

'Yeah,' Lou picked up her phone and swiped through it. 'God, I've got nearly six thousand images on here!' she said, shocked.

She got to what she guessed Callery was interested in, shots of all the students who'd been through the Expression Pod. From all the classes of each year, caught as they came out of the rooms where they were taught, released and ecstatic. Lively and in happy groups coming towards the main doors for another day's teaching, their faces captured shrieking and chatting. Shots of each teacher's classes. Bianchi's, Abreu's, Fischer's, Hayes', Fisham's... Torbet's. Torbet's girls, her cliques. Not just this year, just before she was killed, but past years. One of super-confident girls walking off the court after a game of tennis, sneering or smiling at the camera, in charge of whatever their futures would be obliged to hand them. But then one photo, from four years ago, a group of those same arrogant young women and a couple who weren't so confident. Hesitant, wary of what they were going to be hurtled into. And one particular face, angry, hurt, scowling and carrying all the racquets and a sack of tennis balls, reluctantly landed with a heavy load.

It threw another image back into Callery's brain; a young woman, the same resentful face, scowling and carrying something. He'd passed her, on the boat. She'd been cleared, alibi okay, identity okay. Yet here she was, at this school and one of Jeanne Torbet's students – and on the ferry when Jeanne Torbet died. Carrying unwieldy boxes, unhappy, angry. He'd passed the killer, that soon on after the murder. So soon... too late.

He got in touch with his remote team – there were Courtneys and Madisons and Nats he'd spoken to, they'd supplied the back-up facts he'd needed – but no real relationship had developed, they were just helpful voices completely divorced from what he was dealing with. But then one of them retrieved the info he'd had right at the beginning, names, ages, positions on the staff on the ferry... and he saw who it was. Lauren James, bar assistant. That's right, Callery remembered; she'd been struggling with several small boxes of beer, he'd noticed the lettering. She was still working for the ferry company, thank god; still there to be nabbed. Callery was informed that she would be on the usual route to Calais later the next morning, the early crossing at seven forty-five. He got the quickest Courtney available to make a booking for him and had an early night, disturbed by the fact that yet again he'd be on a boat to France but wouldn't get there.

Callery arrived at Dover, met the WPC he'd requested and the two of them boarded the boat; Callery felt as though he was sneaking onto it. He encountered Steve Spauncey, asked him where she was and was told she was in the back, getting stock. Callery went there, saw this scared, aggressive girl and made himself charge her. In a small office on the top deck he formally charged Lauren James, took her statement and listened to a sad, lost girl.

'I was "out" – and then I was out. Out of the school, out of my home, out of the life I'd known and into an empty, terrifying new one. And it was all her fault.'

'Your parents were pretty hardline about you being gay?'

'No, the opposite! They "understood" – they *forgave* me. Do you know what it's like to live with people – be supported by people, be dependent on them – who think you've done a terrible thing but they have forgiven you? It makes them feel so fucking wonderful about themselves, letting you stay, that their self-imposed saintliness chokes you! I couldn't bear it, I had to get away – but with nowhere to go, no money, no nothing. I drifted, had a couple of useless jobs – got sacked from one for pilfering – then I got – I met Dean.'

The young woman's voice tailed off and she stared at the floor.

'Who was Dean?' said Callery.

'My *boyfriend*.' It was said with a sneer.

'I thought you were— you know, you liked women.'

'I did. But I tried to convince myself that it was – like my father had insisted – just a phase. That I'd grow out of it. And meeting this bloke, he'd put me right, sort me out. He sorted me out all right. I wasn't gay anymore, I was wretched as hell. He made sure of that.'

'How?'

'Drugs. Got me on to them, got me selling them for him, then ended up pimping me.' That set look of utter hate returned to Lauren's face. She looked back up at Callery.

'Now you see why I had to kill her? She'd ruined my whole fucking life, just because she'd fancied a bit of fun. She wasn't even completely gay! She had that rich bastard on the go too, in the background all the time – she used me to fill in with what she saw as some amusing, pervy sex when he didn't pay her enough attention. *But I loved her!'*

Lauren howled and collapsed; the WPC caught her and put her in a chair. Callery hunched his shoulders uncomfortably. It didn't seem right, arresting the victim.

Chapter Thirteen

And after that he had to give Anishka Perry the true story. And relished it; once Lauren had given in and confessed, she supplied so much that Perry should have found out but was too vain and busy to do so. That Moxey possibly suspected but hadn't got around to use.

'I think you should prepare yourself for a bit of a shock, Ms Perry.' Callery explained about Lauren's arrest and her confession.

'Lauren James? But she was so – so happy! So settled and stable and – she was such a good student, her exam results were marvellous!'

'She was a good student,' said Callery. 'Until Torbet got hold of her, seduced her. Underage: you had a paedophile on your staff. Ms Perry.'

'Oh hardly that, surely!'

'If it had been, say, Orlando Fisham and a girl student…?'

There was a long, uncomfortable pause. 'Yes,' Perry finally said. 'Yes, I see what you mean.'

'And you had no suspicions?'

'What do you mean?'

'This clique Torbet had; didn't it ever occur to you that it was *too* close, unhealthy?'

'I— I suppose I didn't pay enough attention to my teachers and their pupils, once they were allocated and terms started. Being head of such a prestigious school isn't just a matter of presiding over a curriculum; my job is very challenging and involves many issues as well as actual educational ones.'

Callery parked that one for a bit later. 'Didn't you think Jeanne Torbet wasn't quite right though?'

Anishka Perry sniffed. 'She was from Paris. Parisians have an innate sense of superiority that often isn't justified, I think.'

'But she wasn't.'

Anishka's eyes narrowed with curiosity. 'Wasn't what?'

Callery had looked forward to this. 'She wasn't from Paris. She wasn't even French; she was from Devon.'

'Devon? *Our* Devon?'

'That Devon, yes. What does Torbet sound like?'

'Torbet – sounds like Sorbet, frankly… Tor— Torbay? She came from *Torbay?*'

Callery nodded. 'Janet Williams from Torbay, parents owned a B&B, she had a brother who ran a garage that did well from MOTs. She wasn't nice, she wasn't gay and no, she wasn't even French.'

'Really? This is— you're sure of this, it's been verified?'

'Yep. We finally got to the truth about her whole background.'

Anishka Perry winced slightly at the yep. 'I don't know what to say.'

Callery shrugged. 'You'll need to say something, sometime. You had an imposter working for you.'

******

That was good, shocking Perry with the real story about Torbet. And now more came out, once the press was allowed to ignore getting through the gates for interviews and could just gnaw on the financial flesh and bones. Stutters had been revealed as not an amazingly successful place of sophisticated and enlightened learning, but a centre of serial lies and deep fraud. The SFO got onto that and everything came out; the siphoning off of vast sums of money from parents and investors, massaged into healthy figures by the complicit accountants and then poured into the off-shore bank accounts of those massagers and Perry.

It had all been fake really, Callery thought as he cleared the papers from his desk. The victim; not her real name, not who she really was. The chauffeur-driven car to the ferry, the booking at the George Cinq in Paris, Torbet's movements and plans had been looked into and shown to be paid, not by a very wealthy woman, just one with good savings in the bank that had all been blown on these apparent trappings of affluence. There had never been any rich lover. Her killer, again not who she pretended to be on the ferry, or at the school; not a rootless young woman in temporary work, not a simple schoolgirl who just admired her teacher. But the teaching staff, too; Hayes wasn't Hayes. Fisham wasn't the eccentric artist he painted himself as, but a grubby member of staff who slept with the Head to stay in favour and, once everything came out, had also been claiming money for years as a carer for two non-existent parents with dementia and a wheelchair-bound sister. As for Perry – not a brilliantly successful head on the way to greater success. All those princes she boasted about – she was just a crook and now she wouldn't be moving on from Stuttenden to fame as a politician; her next career move would be how to survive in prison. Callery shuddered to think how well Perry would do at that.

So, not one of them who they purported to be. It felt familiar; Callery didn't feel like a true detective. He would have solved this case – eventually – but it had taken him too long, he should have worked it out earlier. He should have been on a different ship at the beginning and not had anything to do with this murder and its messy aftermath.

Now he *was* going to be on a different boat; murders didn't happen that often, especially on cross-channel journeys. He would get to France this time, he would have a huge lunch at the first decent brasserie in Calais a taxi took him to. And he would have as many courses as he wanted. But first—

'Ms Moseki? I hope I'm not disturbing your lessons—' Callery had thought about this for a bit, then stopped thinking and just acted, phoned.

'Not at all, I'm just in my study doing some prep.'

Callery gulped. 'Would you like to go to France?'

'I've never been. Every chance I get, I go to Italy.'

'I've never been.'

There was a pause. Not a long one, but long enough to start Callery thinking he'd made a big mistake.

'How long were you thinking of?' Carmen enquired.

'Oh just the day – you know, a day trip, only Calais – I need to exorcise that ferry.'

'A day would be possible. And maybe, later on, a day in Calais could… evolve into a weekend in Rome or Florence, perhaps?'

'Er, yeah! Yes, it could. Do you like mussels, Ms Moseki?'

'I believe they're called moules in France, Inspector Callery.'

'Yeah… they are.'

FIN.

Printed in Great Britain
by Amazon

79508418R10079